STRAYHORN

Books by William Herrick

STRAYHORN

THE ITINERANT

STRAYHORN

by WILLIAM HERRICK

McGRAW-HILL BOOK COMPANY
New York Toronto

to Mary and Anna

STRAYHORN

I

The grave was my benefactor.

Elegantly draped in black silk Italian suit, soft black fedora, white silk shirt ornamented by long, narrow, red tie, I faced the world. Dressed by coin never earned by me, fed by food paid for by disaster. A life insurance policy, a bequest, damages awarded on the basis of mortality tables.

I was death's beneficiary.

Slept in a rooftop flat of a hotel owned by my Uncle Rob, off now with his serpentine Bry on some foreign junket chemically combusting biology with gold and culture. Impeccable though I appeared to the world, my two rooms smelled of human sweat, dirty linen, a half ton of old musty newspapers, unwashed dishes, forgotten garbage, unescaped organic gasses glassed in by the city's grime, for I permitted no maid to enter. It was *my* nest.

Shod in pointed black calfskin—tassles for laces—I strolled about the city, a tall, thin, handsome man of thirty odd, showing it a bored, polished-smooth face. Dark, too, though I saw the world through agate gray.

"Hard as rock," my few acquaintances met at some club or eating spot often said. "Made of stone, the bastard, his heart a polar ice cap."

No controversy there. I had, and have, no heart of gold.

Of stone. No doubt. A great rock, like an unwanted inheritance, lay buried in the very center of my quivering belly. I *was* of stone. Should I have let on otherwise? Buried deep in my interior cave lay the sharp-edged rock—my grief? my conscience? the history of my short-lived life?

I was starved.

After the debacle which destroyed my wife and child and made me wealthy enough to quit my nonperson job, as the sociologists say it, of file clerk, Grade IX, I ran about quite a bit, untrammeled, yet slave to my new-found freedom. I did cry, but it proved too upsetting to Uncle Rob, his wife, and those of my friends nearby. Weeping's old-fashioned, they said. The doctor pre-scribed tranquilizers. Did the trick—not a drop did I henceforth shed.

To escape my grief, I skittered about, fled to Europe, saw the world. Returned, a few more disasters added to my list. It would seem I was death's minister. I touched; you suffered. Discomfiting, to say the least. And, I must admit, brutalizing.

At a party, one of many, I met a girl, an ugly girl with a large pasty face and eyes like those of a fish seen behind thick oculist glass. Her legs were heavy, black with hair, and she was insane for a man. I could see. Be-lieve me, I was a perceptive man. And every man shud-dered upon sight of her. But those enlarged protruding fish eyes probed and dug into every man's very crotch. Perverse, I engaged her. All about us the crowd whirled and gurgled and laughed, the din of a veritable bombard-ment of broken words like exploding atoms, the laughter hysterical and alcoholic, the eyes shining searchlights blind with wet. Debonair, handsome, darkly smooth, I engaged my black hairy beauty against a closet door in a narrow hallway, shoved and pushed by a screaming, pleasure-hunting mob. I shouted sweet falsehoods into her oafish ears, allowing all who struggled past me to impress my slender hardness on her breathless, aching ugliness. Her desire made her weak and only the closet door and my pressing weight kept her upright. She wished me to speak, to say, "Come with me, my love, I want to find paradise in your arms," but I preferred to play her on my spit, this ugly sow, pressing on her, slacking up, pressing, until she almost fainted, her fish eyes popping with piteous prayer. Then as the swell of the crowd seemed almost to burst the walls asunder, I reached behind her to the brass knob and, pressing, twisting, manipulating, got her and me into the closet, into the dark smell of stale carbolic sweat, the door shut tight behind us. And I forced her to her knees. She sobbed with shame as I stood staring down at her in the smelly darkness, an arrogant, victorious smirk creasing my smooth face.

But for me victories were always short-lived. Soon shame oozed in.

Shame was my salvation, and I gloried in it. I stormed about the city to stare daringly into the faces of the men and women, the crowds, the multitudes, daring them to stare my shame down. I enjoyed the sport and gained new victories. They inflated me.

I began to ride the subway trains, each day garbed in a new silk suit, impeccable, enjoying the obvious displeasure of the riders in this their daily grind and grovel. Choosing a likely victim, I'd catch his or her eye and stare intently, challenging. Most would turn immediately away. They were ashamed of their shame. What an odd man, they'd think, how hateful, how shameless. On occasion, though, one would refuse to be victimized, and so, two antagonists, our eyes would duel, iris to iris and orb to orb. Since I willed victory, had a glorious shame, victory my end-all, ultimately I would conquer. *Touché.* Once a fat man, an obvious, shameless victim who proved stubborn, and I dueled forty minutes into Brooklyn. I'll pink your blubber, fat man, I willed. So it was. Deflated, the man conceded to his shame and became ashamed, and I won another victory.

One time it was a woman of my own age, a plump soft-breasted woman, bird-beaked, whose eyes refused to lower in shameful retreat. Wavered a few times, but before I could smile in contemptuous victory, she hardened her will, became stronger as the train squirmed through the underground tunnel like the reptile it was. At times our eyes were blocked off by lurching bodies, yet, honorable opponents, each knew the other's eyes still challenged. *En garde.* And, of course, the weary bodies gone, our eyes were still engaged. Mortal enemies, each filled with loathing for the other, the loathing became more violent as the stations swept by. Lunge! Parry! Die!

When the train stopped at the northernmost reaches of the subway system, we remained seated as the coach emptied, our eyes locked in loathsome combat until the trainman, certain we were insane, insisted we leave.

We parted then, each acknowledging the other's unspoken, courageous shame, like two lovers who had detested a secret rendezvous, each having given without taking in equal portion, yet upon bidding one another *adieu* feeling a sad onrush of great love because neither had become slave to the other's master. Side by side we walked down the stairs without a word, in love (I yearned for love and began to dream), but the bird-beaked woman wheeled to mount the stairs for the down-

4

town train as I continued on. I stopped, unhappy, looked back and saw her smiling sadly at me—better to part now, my love, rather than later loathing.

I acknowledged her sad smile with a sadder smile, and, still lovers, forever lovers, we waved cavalierly to one another and each went his way. No happier, no wiser.

Victories too easily won, I tired of the sport. Besides, I counted them as petty, without adequate satisfaction. So I left my Uncle Rob's roof apartment in the old elegant hotel he owned north of mid-town east, where I'd gone to live after my personal disaster, and rented a room on Avenue B, a narrow room with a narrow bed too short for me, a chair, a dresser, a mirror, for thirty-five dollars a month. A hole. Rats, my co-tenants. I turned the mirror face to the wall. Who wanted to look in the mirror? I knew what I looked like. Enough.

Hungered for something, yet couldn't eat. And suffered from constipation, too.

Discovered a new game. How many days could I go without looking upon a human face? Remained in my narrow room, usually sleeping (never dreaming), during the entire day and most of the evening, leaving it for the toilet only when I was certain my landlady was out. She was a gnarled old frozen potato of a black woman who constantly smiled to show her new bathtub-white teeth. Stealthily, about midnight, I'd sneak out and scurry through the streets of Manhattan. At approaching footsteps I would hide in a doorway, my back arched to the street, until the footsteps were upon me. Dying to turn about and scream in his face, I held myself tight-muscled until his footsteps vanished in the night. Another victory, I crowed, flexing my biceps.

Out into the streets again I stole, the buildings' shadows my sole companions. Kept their mouths shut!

Slipped into the alleys, pissed on the walls, pretended I was a thief making his escape; stalked, chin up, shoulders squared, pretended I was a sleuth. A man approached, a seaman off a freighter, perhaps—sailed the seven seas, screwed the whores of six continents, and now ogled the moon. I waited until the very last moment for his face to become visible, for the game must be played with sport, then dashed into the darkness of a doorway, arched my back. Gone. Another human face avoided. A new victory. Good show, boy! Laughed. Keep it up, Strayhorn. Another week of this shit and they'll cart you off.

The clock's hands whirled in imitation of the earth round the sun, the moon round the earth, my victories overwhelming. David Strayhorn, nonpareil.

I hoarded ennui like an old man his years.

Abruptly the energy flowed again, feverishly, driven for sight of a human face: a smile or scowl, who cared, but a human face. Again I slept nights in my narrow bed and roamed the streets by day: mingling with the crowds, my bread and butter; touching shoulders, my meat; a smile from a pretty girl, my dessert. Bade the old black crone, "Peace," paid her extra to cop one last bathtub-white smile, stopped on the corner to buy a case of Black Label, and called for a cab. Had him drive me to one of the remaining missions on the Bowery, near East Broadway, to give its vomit-smelling inmates their gift. Rollicking, they carried me on their shrunken, drunken shoulders and deposited me gently, as if I were royalty, in my cab's interior, then pelted the cabbie with rotten tomatoes as we drove away.

Atop my uncle's roof, thirty stories above ground, I undressed, purified my soul in a tub, drank champagne, and smoked skinny cigars. Uncle Rob, the office informed me, still hadn't returned from his trip abroad with his shifty-hipped wife. Finished off the hour gazing over the rooftops trying to learn tranquility from the clouds and the stars.

Learned nothing but despair.

Enough of being a rag. Came out of it with a bang. The world revolved on a lead pipe and the guy who held the pipe rolled the world. Here I'd been humping around crying for myself and the world kept revolving on that lead pipe knocking down the suckers to pay off under the arch.

Violence beat in my breast like the frantic wings of a caged hawk. I must vent my ferocity. I'd had it and now I was about to lay it out.

Searched the clubs for Vince Sgobbo's son, a kid I'd known as Bash Balls, for such had been, and for all I knew still was, his craft. Bash, a few years my senior, was the sole living link to my childhood, my infancy, excluding Uncle Rob, who really didn't count for I hadn't met him until my mother died when I was eight or nine, already deep into my decline. Bash and I had a strong memory bond since we had played doctor and patient with little Nora Lynch on Tenth Avenue and once after a movie had intermingled the blood of our palms in eternal brotherhood. Vince Sgobbo, his father, had been a man once seen never forgotten. When you saw him sitting at a marble-topped table in a filthy saloon playing blackjack, you saw a huge man with a great head—a mass of black curly hair over an eagle's beak scourged by intense black eyes like two hammered iron links from a chain. Observing Vince leave the table, you snickered. He would lean down, pull out a little wagon from under the table, and manipulating his tremendous arms like crutches he would lower himself onto the wagon, then roll himself

7

away, and he looked little and pathetic, for he'd lost his legs to his knees in an accident stevedoring a vessel on a North River dock. A jury awarded Vince a neat fortune. He invested his money wisely in mid-town real estate; then, after the war, picked up his family—thick-bodied wife, six beaming buxom daughters—and returned to Naples, from whence he'd come some fifty years before. Bash Balls, his only son, he had evicted, ass and ears, as soon as the boy had come of age.

"*Bestia!* Nogood bum—always a be a nogood bum." True.

Bash, I knew, had become chief punk for a gang which ran a multiple business operation: policy, ponies, pandering, and *shit,* which at a court trial became heroin only after the chemist had identified it as such.

After I chased him down, I didn't recognize him, for Bash, who'd been a massively muscular boy, had become fat and slack, his face like an uncooked cruller. He remembered me immediately. Looked up and down my spine with a jellied scowl.

"Must be selling ass, Davey, wearing two-hunnderd-dollar suits."

"You owe me, Bash. We're brothers. Need a job"

"Wit' dat suit? You puttin' me on?"

"Just for a couple of weeks, Bash. Any job. Ran out of bread."

He looked hard into my agate gray eyes, saw whatever he saw, said, "Sure, kid. I need a driver."

Hired me to be his personal chauffeur; since he had no real need for one, I soon understood my employment to be sort of a status symbol for Bash—a driver who dressed like an Italian prince. I found a banal social existence among the cocky punks who worked only a few hours every night as delivery boys for the heroin distributors,

8

and spent their remaining hours drinking, talking shop, and shagging. Among them I remained silent, hiding my detestation and self-deluding superiority in muteness. Like so many of my peers, the only public atrocities I admitted to were theirs and those committed on my very own self. What *I* did, I had good motives for.

It was a bore. Still restless, dissatisfied, my very conscience became a drag, a nag. I must lower myself into a cesspool, the filth not filthy enough. Some, like the marquis, take themselves to the edge merely for the sake of pleasure. He ate his lady's stool to test the hardness of his erection. I wished to go to the edge to see how deep I could plunge. The desire to degrade myself knew no end. The frustration I encountered bred an even deeper violence which threatened to detonate at the slightest touch. Bash, a canny executive, noticed and ordered me to drive his punks about on their delivery routes—a hotel in lower Brooklyn, The 96 Club, The Red Lantern, The Black Stud—hardly different from a milk route, except all deliveries were made at night, the fear of police and narcotics agents real enough. The men I accompanied were like boys playing cops and robbers. Their games I found callow. They themselves did not touch the stuff; they sold it as one sells groceries, for money. Money they wanted for Ivy League clothes, Sutton Place penthouse apartments, foreign sports cars (their taste was exquisite), and call girls who pretended they were models who themselves emulated call girls. I thought of my companions as more bourgeois than the *bourgeoisie,* members of the new *rentier* class of scientists and artists. Vertical mobility at a standstill. I was superior: aspired to more. Wanted to commit a violence on myself.

The girls I encountered on my rounds with the *shitmen* or after hours when play began were as stamped out as fenders in Detroit, the spectrum of colors, the curved shapes, the gauge of metal equal; thin. I became a gash hound. Every night a different fender. A sudden encounter, the headlights blinding, a tangential look, right—left: gash!

David Strayhorn remained without scars.

I cared nothing for the money, the danger seemed minimal, since to me imprisonment would be a reward, not punishment. Thus my job lacked adequate motivation. A mere dilettante, I was quickly bored.

Spoke to my boss. "Need some action, Bash. You can hire someone from the home for the handicapped to do the work I'm doing."

"Okay, okay," Bash smiled, showing a red tongue like a squirt of jelly in the raw dough of his face. His eyes, like two hazel nuts, measured his man. "Yuh was lying— y'don't need no bread. Just lookin' for kicks like when yuh was a kid. Always lookin' for kicks and thinkin' you're better'n everybody else." He stopped to think a moment, then like a D.A. on cross examinaton he shot out, "Taking H, Davey?"

I smiled at Bash. "No, sir. A stick once in a while with a girl. But it doesn't turn me on. Don't need the stuff. Just some action to make me feel alive. That's all, Bash."

His brain whirled as he sat back in his Swedish-modern executive chair in the basement of The 96 Club, the plumbing from the upstairs powder room gushing behind him. "Davey," he said at last, "you're a loner, not the kind a guy for the junk business—or even the girls, yuh wear out the merchandise. Ha ha. Y'got the makin's for what we used to to call a heister, a second story man. A tight ass, lots of moxie. No sheddin' blood, though." Bash had become a pacifist, except when it came to beating his women. Now he pulled out a little ledger from the

10

drawer of his Danish teak desk, perused it slowly, screwed up his doughy lips, closed his eyes, peaked the fingers of his two hands, revolved his chair so he faced the wall behind him, his fat neck to me. I stood before his desk, waiting.

He twirled about. "Got it, Davey. There's a fat broad who used to be a singer, lives in a brownstone up in the East Seventies. Got lots of dough and jewelry and lives all alone now in the basement. A real gasser. Nothing's exciting like a heist, Davy. All yourself, all alone, doin' a neat job, clean getaway, gives a man deep satisfaction. The first time I did it, I tell yuh the trut', shot a load in my drawers. Honest." He smiled sweetly at the memory. "Real kicks. The gamble? Well, a junk-run, if caught by the Feds, for a first offender cops a mandatory five—breaking and entering unarmed, first offense, wit' luck cops a year 'n a day. Had it set up for months but ain't had the right guy for it. It's not in my line a business nomore. Too risky. I'm too big. We even waxed the locks and made the keys. The broad's a real kook. Goes out every day at two forty-five, duckwalks—Keereist, she's fat—to a concert hall, comes back at six. Plenty a time. Bars on the windows and doors. Dark in there." And he proceeded to lay out the entire job for me, concluding, "All yours, Davey, for old time's sake. Nora Lynch, remember? Ha ha. Grew up to be legit. Married a real sucker, an honest bartender, got ten kids in ten years. No weapons, Davey, not even a knife. Y'know, I'm a guy wit' plenty a moxie myself." Very true. In our childhood days I had known him to be a boy of unlimited courage, and in the Korean war, drafted from jail, Bash had won the Medal of Honor for valor in the line. "But don't leave nobody jazz yuh," he continued, "life in a cell's better'n one in a coffin. I know."

11

I nodded agreement with this banal yet much-battered universal truth. Though I hardly cared whether it was one or the other, still I acknowledged to myself—brave admission—killing an unarmed, taken-unaware human being was a profanity or atrocity I would find it difficult to live with.

I knew.

"A heist, Davey, a loner's job. Guaranteed to give yuh kicks." And he belched out a warranty in atonal counterpoint to a further gush in the plumbing behind him. "If yuh carry it off, don't—I repeat, don't—come back tuh me. That's not my line no more. Want no loft squad meddlin' in my business. Every man to his own trade. Ha ha. I give it to yuh like a gift for old time's sake," he repeated. "Keereist, we exchanged blood when we was kids just like in the movies. And Nora Lynch. Wow!" He laughed so the raw dough of his face rearranged itself into a squashed Napoleon.

"Thanks, Bash," I said noncommittally.

"Don't mention it, kid."

We shook hands, and as I turned to leave he said, "Hey! Maybe yuh can have a doubleheader. Wit' your looks, classy suits, and sweet talk, after yuh knock off the heist maybe yuh can do a con job on her. She's a real fat broad. Lonely. Must be dyin' for a guy. Boy, that's kicks, takin' a sucker. One born—"

"Every second."

"Yeah, that's right. One born every second. Davey, baitin' a line and then hookin' a fish, that's the greatest next to gettin' revenge on a guy did yuh in. Take it away, Davey," he said with a laugh, his fat tongue slobbering over his lips. "I give it to yuh," handing me a key and two neatly typed pages. "All yours."

The smell of the air on my way to the hotel was fresh and crisp. Why not? I asked myself, as I sensually hefted the key in my trouser pocket. Nothing like an atrocity to liven my color tone, stimulate the inertia, perhaps bring a flush to my cheeks. All else had failed. I was fair game for my own brutality. A doubleheader, too. I smiled meanly to myself as my blood *did* quicken at the thought. Bash was a true genius. His rhetoric had been masterful, persuasive. A lone man committing a lone crime on a lone victim.

On a dismal afternoon in mid-January, excitement quivering my crotch, just as Bash had said it would, I slipped into the front courtyard of the brownstone, easily opened the iron-barred front door, then the heavy wood door behind it, and entered a dark foyer which smelled clean but damp. To avoid suspicion, as instructed by Bash, master craftsman, I neither switched on a light nor used a flashlight. It was a very dark apartment, but the day's grayness gave it all the illumination it required. My heart pounded so strongly I was suddenly visited by a dizziness which made me falter, the blood rushing to my head blinding me. I stumbled inside and groped for a chair in what I thought was the kitchen and sat down. My eyes closed, I sat quietly, forcing myself to breathe slowly, to have the quivering tingle and dizziness come to some accommodation with my corporeal self.

When my breathing became more regulated, I opened my eyes and was blinded by a golden tiara sitting in the middle of the table at which I sat, alongside it a glittering brooch which somehow reminded me of one I'd bought for Rosalind in London a long time ago. A girl I hadn't understood I loved until too late—Taggart Stray-horn, my father, looming deadly before me.

I turned my head to examine the room I was in and re-alized my eyes were shimmering from the dazzle of the golden tiara and brooch. I snorted in disgust and trans-ferred from the chair I sat in to another, my legs less wobbly, and stared about the room until I could see. The furniture was old but elegant, antiques obviously, a din-ing room, not a kitchen, with paintings on the wall, one a Renoir of a luscious nude whose pink ripeness illumined a dark corner of the room. Though she lived in this base-ment, true, she must be very rich. Pick up the tiara and pin, must be of precious stones, and get out. You've had your kicks. Bash's word was true. But somehow I couldn't budge. My hands sweated in the gloves I wore but dared not remove. Bash had written the script and I followed every stage direction. Though it seemed silly, I knew it wasn't silly at all, for I could easily visualize those bril-liantly lit white scientific laboratories run so efficiently by the police. As Exhibit 1, your Honor, the People offer these fingerprints just identified by the expert. No objec-tion. Received.

Outside, cars hooted and barked. Looked at my watch. Four o'clock. Plenty of time. I had been assured she never returned before six o'clock.

Realized the excitement had left me and I felt a keen disappointment. I had been too excited in anticipation, as when a man is too excited by a girl he is about to lay and there she is, naked on the bed, back arched, hips raised, and suddenly he has lost all desire. Something else, too— I felt enervated. It occurred to me I might be frightened. I'd observed on my travels with my father during the war, when I was but a boy, that there were men who when frightened became enervated, even to the point of falling into a trancelike sleep as if they'd been hypnotized by the fear. No, not I—fear had always excited me.

Perhaps it was this breaking into someone's home in order to steal which enervated me? It is evil. Think about it. Was having fallen—could it be other than a fall? —into the life I'd been leading, a punk's life, perhaps proof of a fear I never knew previously existed; proof of my cowardice? Otherwise, why did I do this which I understood to be evil? Yes, evil, Mr. Tinhorn. There were certain things Taggart Strayhorn had taught me which stood clearly on the side of right or on the side of wrong. Having been taught thus still lay in my consciousness —yes, even though I'd been behaving like a two-bit punk.

Sprawled, spineless, on the chair, I stared at the golden tiara glittering brilliantly on the very center of the graceful oval of the table. I knew I should move from the chair, pick up the jewels so I could say I had accomplished something, made out, and leave—but a listlessness kept me nailed to the chair. Overwhelming inertia. Not my intelligence—that coiled like a snake alert in a swamp. It informed me this must be why many professional criminals fell into the hands of the police, this heavy inertia, this fear which the knowledge of wrongdoing brought upon them.

Take Shakey Carmello. Thirty-five years old and had been as much in as out of reformatory and jail since the age of twelve. The little weasel made a career of hooking kids on junk. What could be expected of a hood who sold his own children for a thousand dollars apiece? Tina who ran the candy store for Shakey was like a baby factory— she manufactured them, Shakey peddled them. Strange man, Carmello: every time he went to jail, he came out with another play by Shakespeare committed to memory. The latest had been Macbeth. Oot, oot, damn sput. . . .

Two weeks later in the can again, this time for uttering false checks, as it was termed in court. I had gone to the trial out of sheer curiosity, and had sat entranced at how masterfully Shakey had controlled the courtroom. Everyone, including the judge, had listened to him in awe and wonderment. "Your Honor, why does the persecution speak puhjawtively about my Tina? She sired my children. . . ."

His Honor had been forced to cover his face with his hand to hide his smile. There was no doubt Shakey's intelligence had been the equal of any in the courtroom. Yet, there he was, a nasty little hood, never earned an honest dollar in his life, and always being caught and hauled back to his cell. The weasel ate well, grew fat and sleek, read Shakespeare, and paid for his crimes. Released, a portrait of piety, he said, "Even wit' society now; paid my debt." Two months later back in the pen.

I, too, must pay for my crimes, I thought to myself, and be penned. Yawned. Commanded myself to move. Knock down da loot, Davey, an' hike. But my insides, those mysterious wrappings and windings, were now stronger than the brain, just as the mysterious life of a swamp in the end devours the snake whole and writhing in its guts.

My eyes, the signal fires of the brain, closed, squelched by the swamp of my body. The snake fought off the mysterious power of the swamp, fought, fluttered, curled, died.

Now I slept a deadening, thoughtless sleep. Once I was awakened by the frantic hooting of cars caught in evening traffic jam. I made an effort to rise but was nailed to the chair, my head on my arms on the table, imprisoned by a listlessness never before known.

CLANG!

I awoke with a start. Cleared my sticky eyes with gloved knuckles—leaped wildly to my feet, danger debouching on the beach of my listlessness with an attack of frantic energy. Into the nearest closet—cedar, camphor, fur, perfume, darkness. Fear. Shame.

Held my breath. Heard doors closing, heavy shuffling tread on the rugs, light switch clicking, saw incandescent strand under door. Ponderous breathing as coat removed, flung on chair, buttons clacking on wood. Heard a sigh. A terrible sigh of such sadness I was almost moved. Weighty, weary step. Another, and then another. Towards my hideaway—held my breath, stomach knotted; who would be more scared, she or I? Right past my door. Heard a doorknob turn, leather heels on tile, cloth whooshing like a canvas tent going up, click of toilet seat on porcelain, door kicked shut.

I opened the closet door an eighth, a quarter, an inch. Heard toilet noises. Before I tiptoed away, aquiver, remembered to shut closet door, caught glimpse of mink, white sable, leopard, sparkling silver and gold gowns, fifty pairs of sandals, pumps, slippers—the raiment of a queen. Blew them all a kiss, toe-danced past the table, could hear her rising, stretched out my hand for the golden tiara—no, slipped quickly out the two front doors, wood and iron, and fled into the winter night with the deep knowledge that somehow, some way, I must return.

II

Gray the city was that day. Gray the sky. I walked slowly uptown past multitudes of gray faces. Even the elegant legs of the chic classical girls left me gray. Planned a shameful deed on a cripple as I passed the ajar heavy stage door of the concert hall. I heard a heavenly measure. It stunned me. I stopped, leaned against a brick wall to catch my breath. I felt as if I had lost all contact with reality. There were many colors, and the sun, a startling yellow, balanced delicately on a water tower's edge.

My underpinning firm again, I wheeled, energy renewed, and let myself into the concert hall. My eyes saw nothing but the stage on which sat three players in rehearsal: a cello, a violin, an oboe. I sat myself down quietly. Seated in the aisle on a carpeted step was the fat woman, obesity an overflow from the bowl which was herself. Greed and lust had marred her body. Her face was pure—an angel's. The players played and were overcome; they were more than men; they emerged from their own petty souls and empty bodies. They played a sonorous fugue and I was again stunned by its beauty. I felt myself lifted and immersed into the shocking cold of a glacial lake. I cried from sadness. The obese woman turned to me and she smiled. Her teeth in the darkness were as white as the cellist's heart must have been at that very moment. She was beautiful. I detested her.

18

Driven by the fugue and my detestation, I ran from the concert hall and emerged into the shock of the gray city street. But I felt I had been bathed clean, a *tabula rasa;* no mark remained on the slate of my heart. I exaggerate. How could I possibly have been without a mark on my heart?

Resumed my slouch and scurried along the building line, in the shadows. Was stopped in my tracks by a blind beggar. His eyes were flesh, purple flesh turned inside out. He wore a round, felt, porkpie hat rimmed with election campaign buttons and a black leather jacket. A yellow hound led him as he played a harmonica. "Sweet Sue." There was a tin pie pan strapped to the dog's long skinny back. The man's livid flesh eyes stared strangely into my heart to see how much money I carried. Finding my heart bankrupt, the beggar spat and passed me by. I envied the blind beggar. Seeing nothing, he saw all. I was certain his blindness was a trick. Hurriedly I ran after him. Abreast of him, his foul smell struck my nose so that my eyes teared.

"How do you make your eyes flesh?" I asked, injecting interest into my voice.

At first he didn't understand. I tinkled a coin into the pie pan on the dog's bony back and now I received an answer. Ah, yes, said to myself, have to pay for answers; nothing comes free.

"Dropped a match into a pail with gasoline thinking it was water. Whoooosh!" he laughed. "Smartest thing I ever did. Make five times more'n I ever made."

I joined his laughter, almost pleased at his debacle; grateful also for the opportunity to laugh at one more crippled than I. "Are you going to let your children follow in your footsteps?" I asked.

This he mulled over, didn't answer immediately. Again

I primed the pump. Tinkle. Even the dog smiled and, I thought, bowed. "Well," the blind man said, humoring me, I suppose, "I'd like them to follow in my footsteps, but y'know how it is, sons of successful fathers are usually failures." As he roared with glee at my gasp, the purple flesh which filled his eyes dripped sweat.

"What do you tell your kids about the world?" I asked. His answer would prove his credibility.

"Tell'em to mend their frailties, because every man they meet will try to tear them down. Every man believes by tearing another man down he helps to build himself up. So, watch out, I tell my kids. Y'got a frailty which another man can see, you're giving him another toehold for his climb over your dead body. If my kids listen, they'll get to the top themselves. They'll be the greatest damndest beggars in the world. Top notch." He roared again, red gums glowing, resumed playing "Sweet Sue."

Ha ha, a mature man. Adapted himself to his environment. "You have a point," I told him, as he continued after his skinny yellow dog, playing his harmonica, smelling strong. He'd lost too much time already.

As I patted the dog's head with one hand, I retrieved one of my quarters from the pie pan with the other (I hadn't, after all, worked for Bash Balls for nothing) and departed. One unsentimental man deserved another. He'd given me a toehold and my toes just ached to take advantage. Simply must find someone to step on and make use of the lesson I had just learned.

Remembered with an unwilling longing the obese lady in the darkness of the concert hall, so I turned and scurried back to the stage door to wait, fully aware she would soon be out. The sun was down, the streets were cold and harsh gray. A thin, unkempt man in a dirty apron and torn sweater wheeled an ancient baby carriage past, selling pretzels. I bought one and tore it to shreds with my teeth. I waited for my lady. Soon she came out of the concert hall, her obesity monstrous even as against the huge metal stage door swinging heavily on its oiled hinges. Her obesity quaked under the angelic face.

I bowed like a courtier to a queen and took her hand in mine, bending deeply to kiss her palm, inwardly sneering.

Incredulous at this attention, she gazed at me from her strangely quiet eyes. Then with fat fingers she opened her purse and withdrew a small white card, which in elegant type read: *Madeleine Dearing, Opera Star.* I realized that though for weeks I'd noted her arrivals and departures from the concert hall, which was on a line crosstown east with my hotel, she had never noted me, which was exactly as I wished it. Not that it mattered, of course. I told her my name and she nodded, resumed her slow waddle, her flesh quaking, as I slouched beside her, speaking in a courtly tone, wondering why I dallied.

"I was taken immediately by your violet eyes, Miss Dearing." I smiled.

She giggled softly like a girl, finding speech, it seemed, impossible. Her eyes slid over me lightly, refusing to take hold of what must certainly have been mirage, shadow, nonsubstance. Again I smiled, my most courtly smile, and I knew how to smile at a woman since once I had been what I believed to be a great lover. Many women had been mine. Dressed in evening clothes, I had called for them in hired limousines and taken them to the opera or the theatre; afterwards we had eaten in the finest supper clubs, drunk champagne, and then retired to my apartment where we'd made love and in the morning they had refused to leave me. After I had succeeded in ridding myself of them, sending them weeping from my flat, I'd sent flowers to their homes and they'd adored me, beseeched me to see them again, and I had laughed. . . .

Lies, my imagination, a dream I'd had years ago. I no longer dreamt of living in the grand style of a continental lover wooing tourist ladies in the smelly piazzas of our world. But I did naturally know how to smile wickedly, charmingly, so that a hugely obese lady would believe I courted her, fancied her, perhaps even desired her. Soon, I was certain, she would be waddlingly, maddeningly in love with me.

She proved more difficult than I thought possible.

Too long had she lived alone, too long had she seen the patronizing stares of ridicule or pity, and though she giggled girlishly at my courtly smiles and bows, at my softly whispered words of admiration, her heart was too deeply hidden behind the mountain of flesh, in the fleshy vault of her soul, her protective coloration, so to speak; she must be careful, some hidden voice cried to her as her eyes glided over me searching out perhaps a foothold, a sure step, all the while waddling from side to side, her flesh quivering, her throat giggling softly.

What an arrogant innocence must once have been hers, to have allowed herself to be so plundered that now she must conceal herself under this heavy layer of fat. I almost pitied her.

It flashed WALK in green. I put my fingers to her elbow and she trembled like a light airy bird and from deep inside a sigh, a terrifying hysterical sigh wrenched loose from the hidden heart, from the vault of her last remaining possession. My fingers to her elbow, secretly sneering, a cartoon villain, I helped her across the traffic-halted street and her sigh became a shrill subliminal wail which I coldly ignored, paying strict attention only to the impatient, angry honking of the cars, and to the hundreds

22

of thousands of footsteps, to the coughing, sneezing, talking, shouting, laughing mobs all about us.

In the East Seventies, not far from the park, we stopped at her brownstone, very neat, in the basement of which she lived. I escorted her down two stone steps to the black iron grille door, which itself closed on a sturdy wooden door. I asked her if she would invite me in for a cup of tea, expecting she surely would—how could she resist my attentions?—but to my keen disappointment she said no by a violent shake of her head.

I asked her if I would be able to see her again and she heaved her immense flesh in a question. Her heart must certainly have long before been impaled. It occurred to me as she turned away from me to insert her key into the metal lock shaped like you know what that I had not heard her speak one word. Before I could wonder further about it, my mind was distracted by the sight of her from behind. Her immensity was staggering and I searched for pity in myself and discovered none; searched for ridicule and found none. I was completely cold to this quivering beast. Dug deeper into myself, deep, deep, and knew I was lying to myself, vain fool that I was. Because from under the rock, far into my belly, I heard a faint wail.

Was it, I asked myself turning again to her, that she had immured herself against possible injury from wayward stones thrown by hooligans and vandals or was it merely—merely?—that she had become so long accustomed to aloneness that she had lost all desire to accommodate herself to the intrusion of another? Aloneness, I'd long ago learned, was not melancholic boredom—it was being seated in an old easy chair in a darkening or already dark room, eyes, ears, nose oblivious to all, the fantasy-producing mechanism out of order. Try the next booth. I knew. I was not of cardboard, not of brass; I was

23

the son of Polly Strayhorn, a woman who'd been a winsome piece of ass.

The clang of the black iron door revived my attention, but Miss Dearing was already lost from my view as the solid wood door shunted shut with a dull thud. I was alone in the small cement courtyard in front of her doors and windows, all barred by black iron. Alone and frightened. For under that immovable mass in the pit of my belly lived a violent beast. Me.

It was night. If there was a moon, I couldn't see it, the surrounding buildings too close and too high. I scurried into the shadows outside Miss Dearing's black iron-barred corner window. A few feet above me the open street swirled with cars, people, dust, and night. Here in the corner made by window and brick wall I found refuge as I peered into Madeleine's flat. I saw a large piano fill half the room. An old fancy lamp gave off a dim, torn, lacy light. On the floor lay a worn Oriental rug, Asia impoverished by millennia, inertia, and crawling multitudes. On the walls hung pictures difficult to see; screwing my eyes I made an effort and saw some were glossy black-and-white photographs in black frames, flowery handwritten words scrawled across their bottoms. Shortly, Miss Dearing waddled into the room and lowered herself onto the piano bench. I could hear it groan under her; her buttocks and thighs overran its edges. She began to play a Schubert *lied* and then opened her mouth as if to sing.

Madeleine Dearing, Opera Star. *Vanished from the scene* had read the two-column headline a few years before.

She raised her head and opened her mouth to sing, and hopefully my ears strained to hear the beauty of her voice. All her beauty, all her hopes, all her humanity would be in her voice—all to counterbalance the beastliness of her flesh. She—and I—would be redeemed by the never-lost beauty of her voice. I would hear her soul, and between us would be communion. My mouth opened in expectation, my eyes glittered, my lungs panted, my thighs became weak, and in my groin I felt a delicious fertility. Her fingers flew over the keys and the opening music was richly beautiful. Now the voice.

But no! She lowered her head, closed her fat mouth, and stopped the running of her fingers over the black and white ivories. She shrugged and like a volcano shaking itself down for a great upheaval of fire and lava she made preparation to stand from the bench. Elephantine sow. So angry was I, I bit my teeth and shook. I wished to spit into her face. Move me, I wanted to scream at her; move me! No. Coldly I watched as somehow, using her hands and arms like crutches, she managed to gain a standing position, almost falling back only once. I wished she had. I wanted to see her demeaned by her own flesh.

Her feet apart like the Colossus of Rhodes, she stood in the center of the low-ceilinged room and stared about from wall to wall, obviously seeing nothing, just a short fat finger poking at a nostril. This she did for many minutes as I peered intently through the window from my protective corner outside, beyond the reach of the swirling dust and the nasty night, wrapped up in my visions. Nothing now existed for me except Madeleine Dearing.

And from her what? Her immense legs spread wide, swaying ever so slowly (as though she were making out with the wind), she gazed dreamily about, her finger in her nose. She began to shudder and I recognized it to be the volcano shaking itself down again. This time it meant she was gathering herself together to begin to walk. She waddled through a doorway out of my sight. Waited—

impatiently, hopelessly, anxiously (more feeling than I'd been able to reap in a month)—leaning into the corner made by brick wall and house, wondering how long I would remain there, wondering why I too didn't gather myself together so I could return to my own smelly den, wondering why I didn't feel pangs of hunger since I hadn't eaten for many hours, wondering at myself, telling myself to take courage, to direct my life, control it, slip its *laissez-faire* non-existence, this life without will or direction, something less than a leaf, something less than a grain of dust, something without a center of gravity, without a surface to give resistance to wind or time, an echo of those wandering lost days with Taggart Strayhorn through the aftermath of havoc in Asia, Asia Minor, Europe, those wondrously hungry days of my childhood and youth. How long could I endure this nothing? How long could I endure?

Perhaps in another moment I would have dug up an answer to my compound question, but right there and then I heard a sound in the room and I raised my eyes to peer through the iron bars. There was Miss Dearing in an elephant blanket of a bathrobe, gray, with a string for a belt tied tightly so that her flesh fell over it in heavy folds. On her head sat the golden tiara. She assumed a stance in the center of the room, again raised her head, a soprano awaiting her cue for an aria.

And sure enough she raised her hands and opened her mouth and I waited again for the beauty which would most certainly issue forth to give life to my flesh. But there wasn't a sound as she swayed and mugged through the agony of some remembered aria of the *risorgimento*. I could see the cords of her throat expand and contract, her monumental bosom heave, her body rock in powerful sad mime (her style dignified, in no way melodramatic)

26

as from her voice box issued not a sound. From her eyes slipped two sincere tears.

Her mute aria endured a full twenty minutes. At its conclusion she bowed to her audience and graciously accepted its earsplitting silent gratitude for her virtuosity. She bowed again and again for ten curtain calls, on her angelic face smug satisfaction at her deserved ovation.

Cold fury strangled me. Enraged at her smugness, to shake her loose, I slapped sharply on her window and made a false face. The sound crashed into the silence of her room. She started back with an animal cry, then stood petrified with fright. So entranced was I at this visible sign of my successful blow at her pitiable smugness that I was completely oblivious to the tears which filled my own eyes.

Abruptly atremble, I leaned into the dark corner to hide from the world.

Just as my imagination prepared to go off on a savage hunt, from out of the darkness a hand descended heavily on my shoulder and yanked me to, the hand of authority, bulbous-nosed, mean, but authority nevertheless, just what I required to set me straight, a policeman.

I showed him my smooth, beneficiary's face and it was then simple to convince him I had just stepped out of the wind for a moment to light a cigar, one of which I offered him but which, to his credit, he refused. I showed him my wallet stuffed with legal tender and my papers and he permitted me to go. Saluted him, slipped into a cab, and departed.

A few minutes later, drooping, confused with my day's adventures, I closed the door of my fetid, unkempt flat behind me. In the dark, tiredly I undressed, letting my clothes fall where they would, impeccable pretense forgotten. Naked, I padded into the toilet, locked the door on no one, closed the window, pulled down the shade, stuffed towels into every channel of escape and in the dark sat stiffly asquat the pot. Teeth clenched, hands fisted, chest heaving, body trembling and sweating from the mighty effort, I produced no more than earlier had Madeleine Dearing, Opera Star.

III

Dreamless, my brain a void, I slept the entire night and day away. Awoke to the sun dying outraged in the Jersey swamps. Showered, drank the orange juice and coffee, both now tepid, room service had left hours before outside my door. Attempted to clean my hole. Gave up. Just opened the doors to the roof and let the wind run through to freshen the air. Used spit and a soiled handkerchief to polish the glass over the respective photographs of my father, mother, and me taken two weeks after I was born, my naked behind a cherubic cupid; of Barbara and me and daughter Alicia five months after she was born, her hair already like the sun's gold aureole lighting up my black eclipsed heart; and of Uncle Rob Strayhorn, his face a computerized consensus of science, money, and love, with his wife Bry, a polecat and snake, the day they were married. As usual, all but Taggart, my father, smiled up at me. Tag Strayhorn hadn't been one to waste smiles even on posterity. I returned their smiles, reserving for Tag a guilty bravado sneer. Up yours, old boy.

Chose a beautiful blue silk suit imported from Hong Kong, polished my black straight hair, twisted and squeezed a five-dollar bill into a tiny ball, and descended thirty stories to the street. Dropped the tiny ball into the elevator operator's tan cleavage and stepped into a taxi.

So fast and jerkily did the cabbie drive that soon I was ready to be sick on his back. I suffer from a temperamental digestive system. Ordered him to stop, paid him, waved a sickly goodbye. He had dropped me off on Fifth Avenue, near a large middle-class department store. Window-stared at the pert mannikins in their chic middle-class dresses and soon became enamoured of one who wore a gay wide-brimmed bonnet, a slight, form-fitted linen shift (she was on her way to the Bahamas) with large square black buttons down the front. How pleasant to unbutton her. And like the sea, endlessly, would flow Madeleine Dearing, my intended victim, until the world —and I—was inundated with melted fat. Threw her a kiss, discarded my neurotic slouch, jauntily strode south and then east to a club to keep an engagement with a friend, Joe Hardman, who'd come up from the gutter and was now very solidly on the Street.

On the edge of his chair impatiently he awaited me, though he did greet me with a brash, sneering smile under his long Bavarian nose. Joe was a man who lived up to his name—hard, with sharp stone hatchet features, who'd learned to play on concrete playgrounds where the knee, the elbow, and the teeth were weapons, and where a knife was not a toy but a knife. Thirty years old, he had a quarter of a million stashed away, made on the Big Board.

As soon as I shook his limp hand, he said, "Made fifty thou today. Real bullish. Buy when everybody's selling; sell when everybody's buying, that's my motto. I'll make the half before I'm thirty-one."

"Half what?" I asked, not really listening, my eyes on the twirling, jerking, jazzy girls all about us.

"Half a million, Sir Fool. Half before I'm thirty-one, a

cool before I'm thirty-five. At forty I'll be king of the Street."

"And at forty-five, dead from a coronary."

"Ghoul," he whined.

As we ate he recounted dirty jokes to which I gave scant smile. Later, impeccable, elegant, polished stone, I danced with assorted young women the dances of the day, as above us, on the wings of the bandstand, two teenage dazzlers twisted and turned to no beat, making out publicly.

During the night a slender, striped fox without underthings and I took a fancy to each other, and after many hours of churning about in very contemporary nontouching dances, so it seemed everyone was dancing with everyone else interchangeably, gender unimportant, in one grand circle, she left with me for my roof apartment.

She wrinkled her nose as we entered, but after a cognac and a stick of tea apiece, we made dry love under a mellow light, each change of posture like a formal, stylized dance, as Kurtin Paller had so recently warned me in a dark cave in Hamburg.

The fox and I pretended great passion.

"Ah, Felicia, a real gas," I panted.

"A blast, Bighorn."

"An underground movie. Wow!"

In the morning she was happy to go. I no less than she. After she slipped into her knit and gurgled with mouthwash, at the door she said, "Why don't you get this fucking place cleaned up?"

"The job's yours, Felatia—a dollar and a half an hour."

She slammed the door.

No sooner had we parted than she might as well never

have existed, a nonperson, a dog in an alley. Kurtin Paller had been a prophet.

I remained in bed hidden under the blankets, nauseated with myself. I was wraith, ghost, poltergeist. I passed through the world, through people, through broken glass and nothing stuck to my bones, nothing left a mark on me. I stared into the mirror of my mind and found not even a scar of a pimple on my face. No blemishes. No erosions. Like a city pedestrian I had learned lately to avoid collision with the most aggressive vehicles of life. Even time. It was all inside, in my gut. The world must never see, for if it did—down would come the guillotine. I was afraid; there were too many ghosts. But if I carried it inside, I would be safe. Yes.

I remembered a story Joe Hardman once told me about a man who had lived next door to him in some two-bit flophouse. Hooligan though he was, Joe had a keen pair of eyes. Ten years before, when he worked with me as a file clerk, to save money (money was his only love, and he was its slave) so he could go into stocks and bonds, he lived in a run-down lodging house on upper Third Avenue, in New York's Little Bavaria. The landlady was a skinflint old biddy who never gave a roomer a thing until he asked for it, and never cleaned the one toilet used by eight or nine lodgers until they threatened to call the board of health. There was one roomer who kept to himself, showing the world a cold face and never asking for anything. A bitter stink began to permeate the hallway near this man's room. It became so bad every time Joe passed by he had to hold his nose. A time came when the lodgers and the old lady did not see this man for many days. The bitter stink more bitter. The lodgers asked the old woman to do something about it, but she merely laughed. "He doesn't bother me, why should I bother him. You don't like it? Move." But when the first of the month arrived and departed and the man hadn't paid his rent, she hobbled up to bang on his door. She heard a chair scrape inside, but nothing else. She rapped on the door. No answer. Fetching her own key—she had guts, if no heart—she opened the door and entered. There was a heavy crash, followed by a rising crescendo of breaking glass. The man hung from the chandelier stark naked, his neck broken, his penis ajut. The place was strewn with shredded mattress guts, floating in a gushing stream. He had stacked thousands of beer bottles from floor to ceiling, each one filled to the neck with urine, and then boobytrapped the entire place. When she walked in, she tripped a string which sprung his homemade gibbet and those thousands of bottles of piss. He hung dead and she almost drowned in the flood.

Now I wondered. Had Joe been warning me?

Hidden under the blanket, ignorant of what went on about me, I muttered aloud in colloquy with myself. It's time you began to think seriously of your life, I admonished myself. Then laughed. Seriously? One born as I was of a mule and a she ass? Impossible, I heard myself answer, because a mule is congenitally sterile. Ergo, the she ass must have been in cohabitation with a jackass, since I was a fool—in other words, an ass.

The ass, let out to pasture, jumped his fence and wandered into a holy place at the edge of town. Thirsty, he drank the ritual wine, and glory hallelujah became a man.

The man loved his neighbors so assiduously, he found it impossible to stay out of their pockets and their wives. Caught *in flagrante*, he lost his life, and God another soul.

The soul, trapped in Limbo, panicked, lost his nerve and yielded to the Devil. The Devil, satiated, skewered and broiled him, then fed him to his dog.

The dog overate, became careless, and ran afoul of a peasant, who, wary, fed him to his ass.

The ass, suffering heartburn, looked to the heaven and learned from God he was a cannibal. Now he suffered from a guilty conscience and thus again became a man.

Alternately I shivered and burned under the blanket, alternately laughed and cried. I was trying very hard to become insane, thus to come by a rationale for my behavior, but as in all else failed miserably. Thus revealed to myself, an impostor, I threw off my covers, jumped from the bed, showered, brushed my teeth with an electric toothbrush, dressed meticulously, a melody in mauve, and descended in the elevator to the coffee shoppe where I had an all-American breakfast for the all-American price of ninety-nine cents. Left a dollar tip and walked into the street, where a beautiful blond male said to his companion, "Look at that guy, dressed like a nigger."

I turned, bowed, said, "My pleasure. Thank you."

In the days which followed, I found it difficult to stay away from Madeleine Dearing, Opera Star. Her barred windows stared crossly at me many times as I stood on the sidewalk wondering how I'd come that way. But I managed to control my want—which was evil—and slipped away without either peering into her flat or ringing her bell.

Another time I passed the concert hall, saw the stage door ajar, continued to the corner, turned back and slipped in. There on the stage stood Madeleine Dearing, a stage light beaming on her sweaty, angelic face.

The players of the previous time sat off to the wing of

the stage, smoking and chatting, paying no attention to Miss Dearing, as she paid none to them. She merely stood in the stance of a soprano waiting her cue to begin Persephone's last aria. Now I knew I would share with her the rich beauty of her voice and, having shared it, be reborn. My days would renew themselves, my very life would have purpose, my shriveled soul would heal itself and would thrive. I lost myself in the vast black auditorium unseen, and sat in the carpeted aisle as I had seen her do, not wishing to make even the smallest sound of lowering a seat. I waited, my heart expectant, aglow. Madeleine Dearing's name had been famous; the most ignorant had heard her on television or radio or even seen her in the movies. She was still young enough to have retained all her power and beauty, young enough, indeed, not yet to have reached her peak. A few years before she had disappeared from public view for some unknown reason, at least to myself, who kept himself ignorant of the public gossip about the famous or notorious.

Dearing smoothed her bodice, shifted her feet, raised her arms, closed her eyes, cocked her head as though listening to the orchestra for her cue, and forming her lips she let go a note so perfect I found myself imprisoned by its very center as it spread in perfect oval into, over, and about the empty concert hall. Yes, I cried to myself, yes. Move me, my love, I want to cry. The note, a full four measures, reached the walls, the ceiling, the furthest reaches of the hall, almost echoed back on itself, became faint and expired, fell into silence. Entranced, I awaited the following note but none came. Dearing closed her mouth, dropped her hands to her sides, pulled down her dress at her unimaginably tremendous hips, waddled aimlessly about for a few seconds, lost perhaps, and then

35

ponderously hurried from the stage. The players, I had noticed obliquely, all this time had gone on smoking and chatting, giving absolutely no attention to Dearing, as if what had just transpired did so frequently.

Still that one note played about my bones, sifted through my half-dead heart, cracked the awful weight in my belly, adumbrated airy visions in the dark corners of my interior, and, finally, after many minutes of silence, fell to rest.

I knew then I must pursue Madeleine Dearing, I must discover the secret of her silence and must shatter it as an artillery shell shatters a stone fortification. I must free the beauty in her and then free myself from the serfdom of my overwhelming weightlessness. Whether she wished it or not, Madeleine and I were at this moment wed tighter than any double-ring marriage.

Madeleine Dearing didn't know. But I knew.

Sent Bash Balls a braggadocio telegram.

> LINE BAITED STOP FISH HOOKED STOP
> WHAT A WHOPPER EXCLAMATION POINT
> YOUR BLOOD BROTHER COMMA ACE TINHORN

In the days that followed Madeleine Dearing more than adequately filled my mind. Strangely, the more she did the more I began to think of Mother and Dad, that grand old couple, my progenitors. Tag banged, Polly pulsated, nine months later I popped out, the Strayhorn comet, five hundred thousand miles per hour around the sun. What a flash!

Taggart Strayhorn had been an engineer, a big, black-haired cur, tall, dark, and silent, never smiled, let alone laughed, till the very last moment of his life. His last violent breath upon him, he laughed as if he had won a huge wager, I his son the loser. Stared at me, sneered victoriously and died, all two hundred forty pounds of him, muscle, viscera, and brain.

He'd been an All-American tackle at Purdue, from whence he had come to New York to plant pipe under the city asphalt for a steam power and sewage system company. Whenever I came upon an excavated city street, there fully revealed to me in all its muck would be my father's pipeline, his very guts. Sometimes I cried. Will I never escape you? Never, the pipe rasps. Never!

It was in New York he met Polly Romer, my charming mother, a poverty-stricken, talentless actress flat on her back.

No sooner did they stare into each other's radiant eyes than he wished to crush and she to be crushed. She was a blonde with a Victorian configuration, large and sprawling, some fifty years out of fashion. Tag Strayhorn fell passionately in love with Polly and she told him she'd marry him if he would be circumcised, since, as she insisted, his looked like a beagle's, and besides it was healthier. For her he did it and they were married before it was completely healed. Impatient, he painfully banged away and in due time there I was, popping my head into the world, toxic. The dear man took one look and ran all the way to Wyoming (he was a man who never wanted to go home) for a pipe-laying job among the branded cattle. Six months later he returned to find Polly pulsating for a lover.

A puritan, Tag left her and me to become a transient engineer, his lifelong ambition, laying unsmiling underground pipe wherever steam and waste demanded it. As soon as he divorced Polly, her lover abandoned her too. I've long since learned there's nothing a lover likes less than a woman without a husband.

Now my poor blond mama was alone in the world except for me, her very own soul. The Depression and FDR had settled down to remain for a while, and it was a bad time even for the burlesque houses, so Polly found the best job she could in an old limestone hotel with a beautiful green copper mansard roof under which she and I had an attic room. She labored long and hard, did Mother.

The strenuousness of her toil must have slightly un-hinged her mind, for she had a schizophrenic habit of first screaming at me, then cooing into my dirty ear, or whipping me till my skinny bottom bled, then kissing me almost to death. I bear her no grudge. In her old trunk I still preserve a picture of her and me. I was a thin, ratty, tiny boy with a mop of raven black hair and a mean, cor-rupt look on my face. She was a ripe, overblown woman in an overflowing bodice, her head crowned by a wild bouquet of golden mimosa the gene of which had been transferred to my daughter Alicia, dead in her innocent childhood, her bones already parched white.

My earliest memories are of that old busy place where the days were calm and quiet, the sun filtering through the Venetian blinds to stripe the sturdy, beat-up furni-ture, the kitchen white and clean, my mother's and my room under the roof cozy and warm and very bright on sunny days and delightfully musical when it rained. It was in the evenings, of course, the old house came alive with the maids, the customers, and a phonograph playing "Mairzy Doats" or "The Moon Comes over the Moun-tain." There was a girl there I was sweet on, I must have been four, Eunice, a knobby-kneed, long-breasted black girl from Chicago who used to sing a song I doted on:

> Keep a-knockin' but you can't come in.
> Ah hear you knockin' but you can't come in.
> Ah got an all-night trick again;
> Ah'm busy grindin' so you can't come in.
> If you love me you'll come back again.
> Come back tomorrow at half-past ten. . . .

I used to go out into the street on 28th and Ninth Ave-nue and play hotel with my sweet little friends, Bash Balls among them. We would cut up old newspapers to

39

make dollar bills, and then I would pay the hotel lady two bills and Nora Lynch, the girl of my choice, and I would go into a packing-case room of our make-believe hotel in a garbage dump of a lot nearby and have a honeymoon. Finished, I'd leave the room as blue-eyed Nora leaned against the door frame (she was well-coached) and called after me, "I hope you can't piss tumorruh, yuh dirty son of a bitch." It was fun.

They excluded me from the hotel rooms during working hours, from sometime in the middle of the afternoon till late at night, after I was long asleep, dreaming my innocent dreams. The place was noisy with fights, screaming, singing, thumping, and the smell of douche bags and lye and other smells which always seemed to remind me of the color green. Since I was a little boy and the hotel rules were slack—red-hot permissive, in fact—I managed to find myself underfoot and many a time under bed. Oh, what a grand time I had as a boy. Once, peeking out of a closet, I saw a man beating Eunice with an army belt as she knelt on all fours, biting her lips so they were white, tears streaming down her black face, her long dugs swinging frantically beneath her, and I became scared and howled. The scene stopped, frozen, and I wet my pants. Eunice jumped to her feet, those long balloons of hers crashing helter-skelter into one another, and yelled, "Get that little ofay bugger the eff outa here." As everyone knows, women who work in hotels are very sentimental, so soon after her brutal outcry Eunice ran to me and lifted me to her elongated bosoms and I was immediately and delightfully strangled. Ever after I've had a predilection for black women with knobby knees and long breasts.

It must have been very exciting, for the following morning when I opened my eyes under the pointed arch, ogival, of our attic room, I turned and squirmed in my little bed and somehow my circumcised thing became hard and taut like a thick thumb and I enjoyed the pleasantness of it, as who wouldn't. And there lay my mama asleep in her bed, alone, soft and sweet, her mass of blond hair like a sun about her head and face. The thick thumb pulsated so pleasurably I thought how wonderful it would be to play hotel in her soft arms, my head cushioned on her great breasts, and I climbed from my cot under the ogival arch and padded swiftly to her bed. Still asleep, she made room for me under the quilt, hot and soft, and I burrowed my little body in the magnificent softness, my head buried in her bosom. There I rested, my thumb so hard it hurt, and I pressed it against her belly, she still asleep, hugging me to her, all under the quilt wonderfully hot and tranquil, and I fell asleep, too. We slept in a sweet embrace. When she awoke, I did too, still in embrace but, of course, though the pleasure remained, the thumb had retracted into the palm of my underbelly. She kissed me, and we lay quietly under the quilt, our eyes closed beneath the attic ceiling, and I hoped we could remain so forever.

But the pulsating clock moved its hands in its timeless manner and soon Mama made a move to rise, my arms clutching her so tightly that as she climbed to her elbows and knees I hung underneath her, and she laughed. "Silly kid." Gently she released my arms and I lay under her on my back, her breasts softly pendant and sweet above me like large fruit and I clutched at them hungrily. She clucked her tongue and then with an abrupt swiftness which took my breath she hugged me to her, my bones aching with an exquisite pain. Again somehow the thumb was thick. She felt it against her body and laughed. "Silly, silly boy." She tickled and kissed me, my eyes, my nose, my feet, my little hard behind, and I giggled and laughed. Then with a terrifying cry she hugged me to her as if she wished to impress my body onto her own, anneal it, to make me again a part of herself, imprisoned forever in her flesh.

Again she laughed, hoarsely, then roughly yanked me from her. "I'll take you to the park," she said, "to see the animals." But the big voice of Sadie, our hotel lady, yelled, "Polly, get your fat ass down here. There's an early customer."

Mama scrounged her full lips into a snarl and whacked my head so hard I thought it would burst. As she slipped into her robe, I screamed and called her all the dirty words I'd ever heard.

She went downstairs and did dog's work.

V

I pursued Miss Dearing. Pursued in the old sense—the hero (or villain) sends dozens of roses every day, inundates the innocent heroine with flowers, jewelry, invents every imaginable way to encounter her, smiles charmingly when he does, the perfect gelatinous gentleman. Discerned with ease that Dearing was addicted to eating rich and great quantities of food. Villain that I was, pursuer of the innocent, bland imitation of the great movie lovers of the past, I sent Madeleine large baskets of fruit and delicacies, the finest chocolates.

She accepted all my gifts and continued to turn me back at her door.

I would stroll alongside her, she would smile, giggle at my banalities or even at my tender words, unbelieving, I was sure, her eyes shielded by embitterment and sometimes by contempt. She knew better. Knew there was no tenderness, knew there was no honesty, knew there was no unselfishness or kindness or generosity or love or even fondness. She was a big fat woman, could almost be the fat lady of the circus, and this foppish man who pretended to need her and want her was playing some wild, fantastic, agonizing game.

No doubt I was a swine. Was as rotten as a decayed corpse. And I asked for no tears.

43

Never did I hear her speak to anyone—at the concert hall, in the grocery, where she was known and was given her purchases from notes she wrote on brown paper torn from a bag in her kitchen. I saw the notes, written in controlled, self-contained, neat, tiny script: 2 lbs pots, 5 lbs flour, 3 lbs but, 10 lbs sug, and so forth. She was greeted at the grocer's with friendly smiles reserved for good customers, nods, and on occasion, when she turned her large back away, with patronizing contempt. Once at the concert hall a young and exceedingly beautiful girl cellist laughed outright at her appearance as she emerged from the darkness of the auditorium to essay one of her soul-shattering notes; and one of the old musicians muttered a harsh reprimand, something like a cultured "Shut up, you dirty little bitch!" so the laugh froze on very white, small, even, feline teeth. When Madeleine's four measures effortlessly expanded to encompass the hall, I heard the young woman gasp. Ah, even the callow were moved.

Nothing, absolutely nothing ever equaled the effortless beauty of that four-measured note. I heard it every day for a month and never once did my reaction to it weary or weaken. It filled me so every corrupt *cul de sac* of my interior being, every stinking canal, was shaken by it, cleansed by it, illuminated by it. Sores healed. And during the heavenly orbit of that beautiful note I enjoyed fragments of sad, lovely dreams. Oh, Madeleine, oh, Madeleine, my love.

That one note, the hurried waddle from the stage, out into the afternoon crowds, oblivious to the incredulous, cruel stares of passersby, the graceless stroll home, I at her side, and I never heard a word from her. How odd we must have appeared to all who saw us. This fat woman in her old horse blanket of a gray flannel coat

44

buttoned to her chin, the round, pink, angelic face as immobile as stone—even when I made her giggle only the mouth moved, never the cheeks—and the worn silk babushka holding in her wealth of titian-blond hair, those violet, intense, penetrating eyes, and I: what carnival did they escape from? I was taller than she, slender, always elegantly dressed in an expensive suit, fine shoes, fitted topcoat with a velvet collar and soft Italian fedora. After all, I was a rich man. I always wore a red tie, since I enjoy the color and it livens up my complexion, which tends to sallow.

She and I ignored the stares, we were too caught up in our own self-fabricated net.

I pursued her and, slow as she was, it seemed I could gain nothing on her. But one day instead of turning east into her block, she continued on past it and my heart leaped. A change in the habitual pattern implied a small victory at least. I cherished it and pretended not to notice. Where she went, I followed: up the avenue, across the square, into the park. To myself I said, we are lovers.

So it was not a small victory, but a large one. I know for many people love comes easy. A chance encounter, a roguish smile, a touch, into the alley: bang! Easy come, easy go. But to Madeleine and me love came infrequently, and very hard, so it must of course be a big victory.

And I noticed at once that the weather had changed. When I'd first met her outside the concert hall it had been a cold gray winter day. Now it was spring, and a few warm days had brought buds to the dogwood, the red maple, and the plane trees. The green of the grass had become fresher, more alive. I made note of it to her, telling her it made my heart warmer as when she smiled.

This time instead of giggling cynically, sort of a purse of her lips, at my foolish words, she pretended she hadn't heard. That way I knew my words had touched her. I put my hand on her elbow as we crossed the arched wooden bridge and kept it there after we had completed our passage. She breathed more heavily, the way fat people do under exertion, and I suggested we sit on a bench. Still no response from her. Now a small gang of kids followed behind us, making faces at our eccentric backs, giggling behind their hands, and I had to turn to shoo them away. Ha ha, I thought to myself, you're becoming sensitive, a certain sign of life. The children jeered, then ran away. When I turned again to Madeleine, I found her staring at me. Her hands held under her monumental bosom, the dramatic pose of a concert singer, she merely stood in her tracks and examined me from head to toe and back again. Calmly, the tiniest of cynical smirks marring the perfect line of her lips, her eyes, like those scientific electronic devices proposed to explore the moon, touched me here, pinched me there, examined and weighed and hefted my eyes, my mouth, the balance of my shoulders, the veracity of my configuration as revealed by my form-fitting coat. Imperceptibly—only I could see, since by now I was aware of her every movement—she shrugged. Had she like the blind man examined my heart and found it bankrupt? I couldn't tell; the scientific data would have to be processed and then stamped out by computer on a strip of perforated cardboard.

Foolishly, I smiled at her, transferred my weight from one leg to the other, made Herculean effort to transmit the hope in my heart to my eyes for her more easily to see it. She merely directed her bulk to the park exit and I forlornly followed at her side.

When we reached her house, instead of going down

the two steps and then taking the five paces to her door, opening it, and closing it in my face as she had always heretofore done, she partly turned towards me, again examined me with her probing eyes, which I was positive left my body and heart pockmarked and sore; she smiled bitterly, shrugged, opened the iron, then the wood, door, entered, and closed both on my face as I leaped to follow behind her.

I wanted to beat her. Became so angry I grasped the iron bars and shook with all my strength, squealing like a wild beast between my clenched teeth. I was merely splattered by dust and rust and the curious stares of pedestrians.

Still, as I trudged home, I understood I had made an advance. Soon the enemy would suffer grave damage.

The morning of every day in the week that followed, I spent in the large library searching out all references I could find about her—profiles, interviews, critical essays on her musical talent, gossip columns. I would work in the library reference room from nine to ten-thirty and then rush off to wait for her to emerge from her iron-barred basement flat. I followed her in her meandering waddle about the city. She seemed suddenly to wish to seek out the crowds. As I had recently gone about challenging them to reveal their shame, she now sauntered fatly among them, challenging them to beat her down with their ridicule, their pity, their disgust at the sight of her. But it wasn't really the multitudes she was challenging, it was me. How long could I endure the notoriety of her companionship? Little did she understand me. The varied and variable attentions of the multitudes meant nothing to me. Only she was my interest. My target. At her side, the impeccable gadfly, I often would be silent; other times I would talk to her, tell her about my life at the hotel where my mother and I had lived when I was a little child; and once, to solicit a tear from her, I told her how my mother had died at Bellevue from an occupational disease complicated by pneumonia and left me a dirty, coffee-stained insurance policy on which could be deciphered the rings from the endless cups of coffee she'd drunk with Sam Shulman when he'd come for his weekly insurance collections from the girls. Ten cents a week she'd paid for her son David Strayhorn, beneficiary. After she was buried all that remained of Polly Romer had been one hundred twenty-five dollars and coffee-cup rings. "All for me, Madeleine," I said. "She rotted alive, not waiting for the hole in the ground, killed by tiny organisms which like blunted silver arrows tore gashes in her womb and brain. Lived thirty some years and left one hundred twenty-five bucks and me. A stinking waste, eh, Madeleine?"

No tears from my fat lady. She merely undid my fingers from her elbow, faced slowly about to stare into my face, squinting her lovely violet eyes to help her look deeper. To see what? Nothing, I suppose, for she faced forward again and resumed her fat promenade.

Other times I would tell her about roaming the world with my father, making transient friendships with hotel personnel in Bangkok one week, Calcutta another, Frankfurt am Main a third, beginning to buy women when I was twelve, the Oriental ladies of my dreams; or I would tell Madeleine about all I'd read in the morning newspapers, which I had recently resumed perusing, about wars, murders, rapes, wife swapping, muggings, the timeless inconsequential happenings of our planet. Mostly she ignored my presence, though at times she would giggle or smile or sneer or stab me with her violet eyes.

For a few hours each day we either rode the subways, strolled on the boardwalk at Coney Island, or promenaded the length of the theatre and movie district of Broadway, and, on crowded Sundays, the park. Then we would rush—rush?—to the concert hall as though she were in frantic rehearsal for her debut. In the darkness we would sit on the aisle, listening to the practice of a changing cycle of musicians, and, again, when they would break for a smoke or coffee, she would raise her hulk, now with my aid (my arm would sink into the softness of her flesh and I would gasp not from the weight of her but from a prurient delight in anticipation of someday being enveloped, surrounded, crushed by this warmness), waddle onto the stage, and enact her pretense. If there was a doubter in the house, she would sing six measures instead of the customary four. She would let fly, effortlessly, powerfully, shatteringly. There it was—proof, if you needed it. Then I would stroll with her to her home, my hand on her elbow, my heart beating wildly, my groin atingle with the hope that perhaps this time I would succeed in attaining my desired end.

Again nothing. She had resumed her old way of ignoring me, then slamming her doors in my face.

Each morning between nine and ten-thirty I attended at the New York Public Library to investigate at least the public life of Madeleine Dearing. B. 1936 Springfield, Ill. Father, Horace O. Dearing, high school principal; mother, the former Virginia Gaud of Akron, O. Virginia Gaud had studied piano with Mme. G in Philadelphia and had made her debut at 18 in NY's Town Hall with

49

less than moderate success. Lost from sight. Married
H.O.D. 1933. Young Madeleine studied voice and music
with Mme. B in Paris, made her debut as Marguerite in
Gounod's *Faust* in 1956 to *overwhelming acclaim.* Not
only *supremely gifted vocalist,* but a *unique musical in-
terpreter, an artist.* After successful tour of the concert
halls of North and South America and Western Europe,
she accepted the *inevitable contract* with the Opera. Always had difficulty with her weight but had obsessive
discipline and constantly dieted and exercised. *Adulated*
in Milan, Paris, London, New York, San Francisco, Rio,
Mexico City, Barcelona, and Leningrad. Private life was
completely concealed from public view. At 25, married
Brian Lorimer, 53, philanthropist, patron of arts. *No
scandal ever touched them.* Several years after being
married, upon conclusion of opera commitment at La
Scala, she and husband left Milan in complete privacy
late one night *to see Europe like regular tourists,* her
manager said; not even he knew where they had gone.
Rumor saw them in Amsterdam, in Paris, in Venice, in
Rome, but rumor never substantiated.

Four months later, in November, she appeared at the
Opera in New York as per contract to rehearse in Verdi's
Otello. To the *company's consternation,* she duckwalked
on stage a good two hundred fifty pounds, covered to her
chin by a buttoned gray flannel overcoat, sang one perfect note for four measures, shuffled about dazedly for a
moment as one lost, waddled from stage. Disappeared;
front-page mystery for three days; page 13 news item for
week; forgotten. Her story revived for few days three
months later when item appeared that Brian Lorimer had
been killed in a tiger-hunt accident in Bengal.

Madeleine Dearing, all two hundred fifty pounds of

her, began to be seen on streets of New York about eighteen months before I began my investigation, at which time she also began to make her momentary appearances in the concert hall. A newspaperman tried to piece the story together but gave it up to go to Washington to write speeches for a senator from the Mountain states. History waited for no man or, for that matter, fat woman. End of news story.

P.S. She was wealthy and owned half the houses on the block on which she lived.

Among the news reports and magazine articles were numerous photographs of the *distinguished Mr. & Mrs. Brian Lorimer.* One struck me with its clarity—a picture of Madeleine standing alongside her husband before a bank of flowers in Kensington Gardens, in London. She was a tall girl, opulently curved in a scant summer dress, a fine gentleness in her face, a lady—so much the lady a man's first impulse would be to want to bring her down, this high-and-mighty, beautiful dame. Lorimer, too, was tall, garbed in a tight-fitted English suit, which he carried off with a long leanness, his head large, strong, and gray cropped; not a hair was missing, his nose straight, flaring at its base into delta wings, beautiful lush mustache and beard. His eyes even in the newspaper photograph stared intensely, so intensely I fidgeted in defence against being nailed by them to my chair. He gave the impression he was a man of indomitable, obsessive will, centered too consciously on himself. His lips were pressed into an askew sardonic smile. Everything about him portrayed a whiplash strength—yet, at his strong mouth there seemed to be a tremor. I stared long at his face and was overcome with an intuitive sense that the man was flawed; worse, that inside he had been eaten hollow by some worm. I looked hard at him. Was that me beneath the beard? Shaven, would Brian Lorimer check out as David Strayhorn? Who knew? My eyes focussed on her. What a young beauty she'd been. Remembered her as she was now. Poor dame. Again examined him. Somehow, somewhere, I guessed, he'd let her down.

Mystery.

VI

Obsessively, urgently, I continued my courtship of Madeleine Dearing, singer of one four-measured note, otherwise mute.

One morning, everything else having failed to arouse her lust for me, I decided to disguise myself and wait for her across the street from her house. At eleven precisely, her door opened and she appeared. Immediately I could see my absence had affected her. Her hands fluttered about out of control, she bit her nether lip—a succulent lip it was—and her eyes searched frantically for me. I exulted. My heart beat fast, my skin stung, my poniard pointed as I observed her from behind my disguise and several garbage cans near which I loitered, an escapee from a Bela Lugosi movie. Her despair yielded me violent pleasure. Oh, how I would have loved to put the dagger to her. Behind my dark glasses and false beard I swelled and beamed. In my heart a hot orange light glowed as in a De Mille movie the sky grows when God is pleased at what is happening on Earth, when His Son has been honored. *Her* despair gave *me* peace on earth.

Now I knew I had begun to penetrate the stone cell behind which she dwelt. I could see that her heart, immured, buried, cemented in under that ton of flesh, quivered at my absence. It took her a full twenty minutes to gather enough strength and energy to turn about, reopen her two doors, and literally stagger back into her dark basement rooms.

When I was certain she would not again emerge, I slouched across the street in my disguise, slithered down the two steps and, pretending to use the corner near her barred window as cover against the wind so I could light a cigar, I glanced into the front room. She sat on the piano bench hunched over, her fat arms clasping herself in an embrace of utter defeat. Behind my actor's beard and glasses I couldn't restrain the cold, harsh, cruel smile of victory.

She missed me.

I became swollen, gorged with blood—so stiff and hard I could have battered down the gates of Troy.

Three days running I replayed this scene, becoming more expert in my villainy each time, and she in her despair. At last unable to control my desire and joy at her utter defeat, I removed my glasses and beard, stuffed them into my pocket, then boldly stared into her window, rapping it sharply with my knuckles until I roused her from her woe. She gasped, and almost fell fatly to the floor as she attempted to stand. Finally, after a few moments of elephantine frenzy, bumptitty bump, she regained her equilibrium, disappeared from the room, and shortly thereafter opened the wood and iron doors without stepping out.

I understood at once: she was inviting me in. Ha! I twirled my unseen mustachios. As I squeezed past her in the tiny, narrow space left to me I gazed into her violet eyes. Her pupils were dilated, her face dough white, her lips open, moist. In my wisdom and great knowledge, I recognized the symptoms of controlled hysteria. I would touch her with my swollen snake, she would fall flat on her fat back, and I would have my way with her.

How my hard snout would luxuriate in that trough.

As we sat in the front room surrounded by old pictures of Madeleine Dearing, Opera Star, in the costumes of the various operatic roles she had played in her great days just a few short years ago, facing one another, her eyes intent upon me, two still violet pools concealing quicksand, I smiled gently, tenderly. Oh, I had once been a gentle man, as tender as any beast. And I felt gentle and tender towards Madeleine as I had once felt towards Eunice the trickster with the long black bubs, towards Polly Romer, my mother, smelling of stale gin under our lovely ogival arch on a rainy day as the weather played a lyrical fugue on the green copper mansard roof, and toward Rosalind, my young sweet love, and Lillian too. But now melting with sweet love in my heart for Madeleine, I wore my smooth harsh face as earlier I'd worn my actor's beard. Why? Why did I pretend? Why must I mask my tender sentiments with black sneers and leers, an incredible gargoyle? The truth was I felt cold and broken and estranged. History lunged at me with its brittle tin bayonet. Power lobbed Molotov cocktails at me from all sides in a hurry to set me aflame. Sentimentality escaped its plastic bag and invaded my nostrils with its noxious vomit gas. Too often had my heart been reached via an attack on my crotch.

So sitting before my fat lady friend, I found it difficult to smile gently at her since I wasn't an actor. One smiles gently only when one feels gently disposed. But perhaps my smile *was* gentle because I realized there and then a gentle emotion at the sight of this terribly obese and mute lady's agony. Staring at me, her face angelic, her

55

eyes simultaneously hopeful and frightened, she wrung her hands.

Yes, it was apparent I had reached into her by force of my stubborn, cunning attentions and was now capable of doing her harm.

Is that what you want? I asked myself. Do you want to injure her?

Without hesitation, I answered myself in the affirmative.

But why?

Because I knew the sole way to revive feeling in myself was to receive the reflected pain of another. I was stronger than she (or at least so I thought); I was more evil than she—though, I'm not to be misread, there is plenty of evil in hopelessness, in weakness, in accepting the role of the vanquished. I was stronger than she because my evil and need were greater than her despair. Thus, there was hope for her—but what for me?

Yet, it wasn't completely an unfair duel, because she had a tremendous defence: she was already familiar with madness—her controlled hysterical eyes betrayed her— and I had only made a casual acquaintance with that ancient but still sturdy and agile gentleman.

Beware the seemingly defenceless! I admonished myself. They use hopelessness to disarm and then the attendant power attained to make order out of their own chaos. How else does one force limits on oneself, how else does one perpetuate oneself?

I knew I had to exert power over Madeleine Dearing —had to order her life so I could then order mine.

And I had power over her. She sat before me cowed. A poor pun. She sat before me not because she wished to, but because she had to. Which proved my power was great. I decided then to use my power. But before I would touch her with my swollen snake and have my way with her I wanted her to say my name. I couldn't bear the thought of having a woman who wouldn't say my name. How then could I—I—be possessed by her?

Looked across at her sitting heaped in upon herself, her agonized eyes searching my face. "Madeleine, my name is David Strayhorn. I want you to call me David. I want you to speak to me, to speak my name."

She trembled, her lips, her entire body—a whale thrown ashore by a storm thrashing about in a frenzy. Her eyes pleaded with me to retract my demand. I remained adamant. I could see the cords in her throat go taut under the effort, her mouth open, her tongue aflutter, panicky captive of her throat.

No sound; she was dumb.

Sweat beaded her forehead, her hands shook, her overwhelming bosom panted with effort like a horse after a hard, parched, uphill run. Her eyes were those of a beaten beast. They gazed deeply into mine and pleaded for surcease.

She almost moved my heart, but I steeled myself. My very life was at stake.

"Say my name."

Her eyes dilated, she kneaded her lips till tiny drops of blood appeared, the angelic passivity of her face took on minute twitches, her hands tore a handkerchief to shreds, her awesome body squirmed in agony.

The greater her agony, the steelier my eyes became. "My name, please!"

Useless. She dropped her eyes to the floor, sagged further in on herself, lay on the chair a hopeless sack.

I wanted to kick her. My cruelty and her hopeless agony made me impotent: my snake shriveled and lay as dead under the rock in my belly.

"I'm hungry, Miss Dearing," I said to break the impasse.

Her face become soft, an angel's, she smiled, her fear relented, and her spine became upright. Her lovely eyes looked adoringly at me. Now I was her savior, fool that she was.

She began what for her was always a struggle, to rise to her feet. I went to her and grasping her arms helped her to stand.

Now we faced each other, close, intimate, we could smell one another, feel each other's breath, our bodies touched at each inhalation. We searched and probed each other's eyes, we breathed deeper, less controlled, a little wildly. In my heart I felt great pain and in my center monumental desire for her. We placed our hands on each other's shoulders.

I saw her desire was as great as mine, greater perhaps, but that she wouldn't permit me to have my way with her. Her eyes were of extraordinary beauty. No frivolous beauty—the beauty of profound wisdom, of deep knowledge. Looking into her eyes, I could believe she had been born with this knowledge, but of course it wasn't so. What her eyes seemed to reveal to me was that she had known corruption and had learned to reject it, but in rejecting it she had totally subjugated her heart, had immured it in a ton of flesh. They, her eyes, were sculptured deeply under her forehead, an unmarred white marble, broadly spaced and straight, the violet firm with a splash of blue which was heightened by the glint of my red tie reflected in them.

We stood closely, and I saw her eyes now didn't falter, they looked deeply into mine and it was my turn to be afraid. Could she read me? Could she see the worn threads of my life force, their decay? I wanted to run away, but her eyes held me, not captive, as she held her own heart, but upright, just as my hands had only a few moments before helped her upright. Was it possible that I loved her? This fat clod?

I was intimately close to her, and she had a clean smell and her hugeness wasn't offensive to me. It had a tremendous strength in it and I had an urge to be enfolded in her arms and to be lost from view. For I was possessed by an indefinable fear, as if my entire life was at stake.

But it held only for a few seconds.

Slowly she turned and trudged into the kitchen. I sat in the soft chair and smoked a cigar, forcing my mind into an aimless path, staring glossily at the black-and-white photographs of Madeleine Dearing as Desdemona, Ariadne, Lucia.

But my mind refused to be sent off aimlessly on some becalmed leaden sea, ignorant of thought. What was the corruption she had known? Had it been so disgusting, so offensive, that her only defence was to submerge her heart in a carload of fat? Had it been so venal that to give it freedom would mean to permit venality to thrive? Was she held captive, as was I, by the conflict between relative liberty and *some* venality and total subjugation and *no* venality? Isn't total enslavement, I asked myself, also total corruption, therefore more horrible than *some* corruption but relative freedom? What had happened in those lost months with her husband Brian Lorimer that had sent her heart scurrying into a cubic yard of carbohydrates and slit her tongue in two? Some *stupid, human* vice, no doubt. She had probably conceded to a human frailty and become so incensed at discovering she too was human that she'd lost touch with the most human of the senses—seeing, hearing, smelling, touching, thinking. Only hunger never loses it magic. For soon Madeleine

59

appeared in the doorway—filled the doorway—and with a curt nod of her head beckoned me.

Before us on the table were a platter containing a tremendous cheese omelet—perhaps a dozen eggs had been used—a large basket of Vienna rolls, and a pot of hot coffee. We set to silently. Excellent. She ate most of the omelet and ten heavily buttered rolls (I counted them); still I must acknowledge she ate with grace. This fat cow, this obesity, ate with grace and elegance. Her hands, I saw, moved with lightness; even in their fatness were they light and graceful. Since we spoke no words, our eyes must do the work of words. So I ignored her capacity for food, her hugeness of body and saw only her face. Her lips were sensually thin and dark red, her chin had length and roundness, and her cheeks in her oval face were firm and smooth. But her eyes, her violet eyes under the graceful abutment of her forehead, they were a mix of cynicism and gentle sagacity. They read my eyes and beyond, and I wondered at them. Would I ever learn to read her eyes? Fearfully, yet hopefully, I wondered if I would ever have the easy pleasure of reading the trivialities in her eyes. As I sat wondering, reading her face (reading the important things easily, simply because they were important and large, thus easily, simply read), she rose from her chair and waddled round to where I sat and stood rigidly at my side. Frightened, I looked up at her, almost, but not, saying, what the hell do you want from me, I'm the chaser, not the chased, when with a quick movement she raised her hand and ran her fingers tenderly through my hair. I felt nausea rise to my throat from her touch so full of fear was I, and I was certain my fear stank to the arch of my very own dome, but she didn't seem to mind, just continued to run her fingers lightly, tenderly, through my hair. I became rigid. Still she pressed my head forcefully to her breasts, and a groan escaped from my lips. I was repelled—and yet utterly enthralled. The smell of her was sweet and clean. My head sunk deeply into that wondrous swell, my eyes looked upwards into her eyes staring down at me with profound concern, yet with a faint touch of cynicism as if she'd read every falsity which like neon lights blinked off and on. I was afraid she'd see all those busted bulbs. Again running her fingers through my hair, she began to hum a strange tune, stopped suddenly, unclasped me, and waddled to the other room as I continued sitting, caved in on myself. What did I want from this woman?

And what was it she wanted from me?

I permitted the torn fragments of a thought to enter my mind and to take root: whatever it is has to do with life or death. And I am death's beneficiary, am I not?

Soon she re-entered wearing her gray flannel coat. The clock on the wall read 2:45. I understood. So I rose and left the apartment with her and walked through the city streets, this time as quietly as a stuffed parrot.

A famous Russian violinist rehearsed at the hall and there were more than the customary number of toadies about. Of course she was known to the virtuoso from Kiev. She and I sat together on the carpeted aisle, in the dark, touching with our shoulders and buttocks. She felt, I thought, unusually taut that day. Her moment arrived, the violinist stepped into the wings, she slowly rose with my help and ambled her heavy way to the stage.

Took her stance, raised her arms, pulled back her head, and rang out her one note, this time, however—we make progress!—holding it for a good eight measures. Its beauty ran like a knife down the length of my back— sharp and threatening, like the honed blade of love.

When she had concluded, the violinist strode from the wings and bowed to her. Her smile was that of a queen acknowledging her due from a serf. She returned his nod with one of her own, majestic and arrogant. There was an arrogance in Madeleine as though she had an image of herself as someone more than mortal. Observing her then, the thought flashed through my brain that perhaps it was this very arrogance which had led to her disaster. But I also felt pride in Madeleine at her conquest. I ran quickly from the hall to the florist next door and bought her a single white rose which I presented to her as she walked from the wings of the stage. She held the rose to her heart, took my hand to her lips, and kissed my palm.

Her lips burned.

My very soul shimmered in her burning flame.

Into the twilight of the harsh street we marched. The buildings stood in gray and black shadows. The windows shone with a pinkish lavender from the sinking sun reflecting off rain-laden skies. It was April. We proceeded arm in arm towards her basement flat. On occasion she had to stop to catch her breath; I was a fast, impatient walker, and it must have been difficult for her to keep pace with me. For the first time since I had begun my conquest of her, as we walked she took my arm and held it with all her weight, almost clutchingly, dependently. More, she took my arm possessively. As opposed to the feeling of fear and nausea which her touching me tenderly had earlier evoked, now her possessiveness made me wish to fly—to soar. I wanted to be possessed completely and wholly. Tenderness and love, I knew, required a responsibility which I had not as yet the energy to summon. I needed first to be possessed and to possess, otherwise I knew I would die from mere lack of energy to live.

And now Madeleine held me so endearingly, so possessively, that I should have been filled with joy, with impatience at the approach of her door.

But no! That would have been simple, and I was if nothing else a perverse man. Instead of entering with her, I stopped at the threshold and advised her I must leave.

Her body sagged and her beautiful face became haggard from chagrin. One of the pleasures of being possessed is the chagrin so easily inflicted on the possessor. Thrilled that my leaving pained her, I insisted I must go, I had business to attend, an engagement. It was simply now I had cracked the wall in which she was immured that I must escape and not enter. What I had most wanted I now wanted least. Overcome by ennui, I must retire.

Madeleine held my arm tightly, pleaded with her eyes, which only made me adamantine. "I'll return tomorrow, Madeleine. I've got a date," I lied.

Abruptly her feelings were lost from view, her eyes awash with cynicism. She was tougher than I thought. Now I wanted to stay, but realized I couldn't, my game would become obvious to her.

I shrugged, kissed her ring finger, tasted the cold of her wedding band embedded in warm fat, and fled. Somewhere behind me I heard the clang of iron and then thud of wood against the jamb.

VII

Deserted. Afraid. Unpossessed. Enervated.

As I shambled homeward, I knew in order to regain some energy I had first again to learn how to possess and be possessed by someone who was alive, though mute and fat. Possessed, I would find it impossible to feel deserted. Overwhelmed perhaps, but never deserted.

Once, shortly after the violent deaths of my wife and daughter, two kind friends, having observed my chaotic existence, invited me to go with them to a strange city on the West Coast. They had business there, the matter of a movie script, and they asked me to come along for the ride, just to have something to talk about, to go three thousand miles, attend a business meeting, eat lunch, return the same day in time to eat supper.

After our whistling arrival, they ran off, first asking me to meet them several hours later on something they called The Strip, a restaurant there.

It was a huge sprawling city, to my eyes ugly—hot, ugly, strange, at least where I walked. There were sections of the city which were beautiful, I was told, but I couldn't find them. As I ambled along on the burning asphalt inhaling noxious carbon monoxide and butane gas, I began to feel totally deserted, alone—the boulevards were very crowded with people and cars yet I felt I was alone on some dry, hard, desert road. I could feel panic taking possession of me.

Get out of the sun, I ordered myself; find an air-conditioned bar and have a couple of beers. But no, my despair was like some preternatural device which kept me walking the burning streets, among these unfamiliar people, starkly alone. Turned a corner and was confronted by a man of extremely short stature, a dwarf, a midget, a gnome, call him what you will. He had a large head on a tiny stringy body, wore floppy purple trousers, Mexican huaraches, a carmine sport shirt. His nose had the shape of a shrunken lung.

He blocked my path—a grin revealing widely spaced, pointed teeth, as though still another mistake had been made along with the others by his creator and his teeth had come out doglike. I apologized, and moved to go around him. But he followed me, skipping lightly, and confronted me with a doglike grin.

"Excuse me," I said, not a little impatiently.

"Hullo, mister."

"I'm sorry, I'm in a hurry," I lied.

"You look sort a bushed," he sieved through his teeth, not unkindly.

"Perhaps I am," I said, weakening, lonesome.

"Buy me a drink," he said, his voice rising from his heels, and though for him that wasn't too long a way, still it was as low a basso as I had ever heard.

I extracted a dollar from my pocket. "Sorry, but here, buy yourself one."

He laughed and it was like the growl of a hound. "Haven't you heard," he asked, "drinking alone's bad fa yuh? Come," he said winningly, "my house's just around the corner. We'll have lemonade." He merely wanted company, I could see.

Just this brief interchange and I felt better. What could I lose going with him? I was twice his size, and, besides, it was almost a kindness. I did have my human moments.

We walked a block east, rounded a corner, and came to a street lined with what I can only call frayed palm trees, worn and discarded from some movie set, or so it appeared. We stopped before a house built to his proportions—a dwarfish house for a dwarfish man. I pretended not to notice. Bending almost double, I managed to enter with him into a clean, tiny place furnished with children's rattan furniture.

On one wall hung a huge blow-up of a movie still of Lon Chaney dressed as a woman wheeling a baby carriage from which what seemed to be my friend's face shone out under a baby bonnet. Alongside hung another large picture, one of him standing close to the fat woman of the circus, mountainous, and on whom had been drawn with a pencil two fat nipples and a black hairy twat. It seemed he had my predilection for fat women.

He motioned me to a man-sized chair, the only one in the room—I felt as though I'd been stuffed into a doll house—and I sat down. On another wall were tacked stills from *Snow White and the Seven Dwarfs*. Was he Dopey? In a corner squatted a television set, on, but with the sound turned down, and while he was in his tiny kitchen making us lemonade I watched a silent daytime serial.

"Have it on all the time," he said, entering with two tall frosted glasses of lemonade. "Keeps me company. Hard to find company. Who wants to be seen wit' a dwarf? Nearly all my friends is dead. I'm over sixty-five." Said proudly.

"I wouldn't have figured you to be over forty," I said, incredulous sipping the refreshing lemonade.

"Because I'm little. Little guys always look younger. Fat people, too. And niggers. It's the skinny ones look their age. Full of wrinkles."

For a few minutes we watched the television program.

"You see that bitch," he said, pointing to a haughty young blond girl on the silent screen, "if I was her parents I'd whip hell outa her. She's the mother's daughter, the guy's stepdaughter," referring to a handsome, clean-cut, middle-aged, white-as-milk couple on the screen, "and she went and stole her stepsister's husband. The stepsister's the man's daughter and his second wife's step-daughter. Ketch? She's a goddam bitch, but I'd like to throw her one." To him they were alive and true and he lived every moment of their lives with them. "What you doing in L.A.?"

I told him.

"Big shots, eh?"

"Trying to be," I said, showing him I was on his side. "What do you do?"

"Used to get bit parts in movies. Once played with Lon Chaney." He stared, and I with him, at the blow-up on the wall, and we were silent as his mind did a backflip to the days of his greatest glory. I stole a glance at him and saw his face had become pink and his eyes wore a look of disbelief at the sight of himself sporting among the gods. Then he sadly shrugged his shoulders and closed the vision out with a quick blink. "But my parents got me this setup. Soon's I was twenty-one they built this house for me and kicked me outa theirs. Didn't mind. They was ashamed a me and I hated'em. Mutual. But they left me conscience money. Wit' money I could always get a dame. Still can. Midgets is always hot in the pants. My wang's as big as any man's. Midgets can do it all the time. Midgets and niggers."

"I'm glad," I said. "Especially since you both always get the short end of the stick."

He laughed, pointing his canines at me.

"But I gotta good friend," he said, "the best," rising on his stringy little bowlegs and going to another room. He returned with something cupped in his hand, a white plump mouse, as it turned out. He must have fed it milk and honey, so plump was it. It ran up his thin little arm, ducked under his open collar, rummaged around his body, emerged from his short sleeve on the other arm. "I call her Bette Davis," he grinned, his fangs showing. "Look, she got popeyes."

True, the mouse had pinkish popeyes and a fat pair of loins. Without trying hard, I did find the mouse resembled the movie star, who really wasn't my style, having starred before my time. These days we like our hysterics cooler and prettier.

Shorty, which of course is how he referred to himself, and I watched the silent TV in silence.

"Bette," he growled between his canines a few minutes later, indicating his mouse, "owns me and I love it. We own each other. She holds on to me like hell wit' her little feet. Wit'out me she croaks dead. Wit'out her I go buggy. Just the television and the smog and all the damn niggers round here."

I looked at him.

"Well, they gotta right to live," he apologized, "but why round here? Knockin' real estate prices down." He kissed his white plump mouse, drank his lemonade, closed his eyes, and patted Bette on her fat loins, a beatific smile on his thin face under the shrunken lung of a nose.

Had to meet my friends on The Strip soon, so I thanked him for his hospitality, he had been kind to a lonely man. But Bette was snuggling in his hair now, preparing to have a hysterical scene, no doubt, and his eyes were still closed, in happy, possessed and possessive repose. He was in his very own home, with his very own love, and his very own memories. I no longer existed for him. And, believe it or not, I envied him so much his home and his love and his ancient glory, that my own heart became gorged with bitterness. In retribution, may it be said, even bent double I hit my head hard on the door frame going out.

Now as I shuffled southward to the filthy nest where I slept, forlorn at having repelled Madeleine's wish to possess me, to give me a home in her lush, warm breast, from the memory of Shorty and his plump, popeyed mouse, I slid into another memory, of the freed Ukrainian miner, another transient friend of my past.

After my mother died and left me one hundred twenty-five dollars insurance money, my uncle Rob Strayhorn, a biochemist of note, who even then knew how to interbreed the two cultures of science and economics, invested the money for me so wisely it became in time the cornerstone to the edifice which now houses my modest fortune. Rob also sent for his brother Taggart, my perambulating pop, who came and carried me off to see the world through hostile, scared, and embittered eyes as he laid pipe for the United States government in the devastated wake of war.

I was a mean little boy who walked about with his back arched like an alley cat ready to spring and his claws open, and my father was a black-haired powerhouse who beat me every opportunity he had. "Keep your spine straight and look me square in the eye. You're *my* son." As if he really didn't believe it.

We island-hopped after our victorious armies, laying pipe. It didn't, of course, take long for me to become accustomed to the sight of shattered bodies, high piles of corpses, and the bloated bellies of the starved. Though we ate relatively well and the hard signs of constipation revealed themselves. I liked only to move my bowels in clean toilets and they were exceedingly difficult to come by on our wanderings, so I saved my wastage as a miser his gold. The hungry rats and hands of lonely men I learned to fight off with my fists and hard curses.

Tag Strayhorn taught me how to read and write and gave me whatever money I required for food, clothes, and the young ladies of the Orient, Singapore, Jakarta, New Delhi, where sexual love begins before you're ten, and I was considered retarded because I didn't pop off till I was twelve. On the banks of the Perfumed River near Hue in Indochina, in the mouth of an eleven-year-old whore at the very close of the war in Asia. I still can remember the exquisite bite of her tiny pearl white teeth as I sprayed for the first time my joyous seed in her hot red mouth. For ten dollars I fed her and her multitudinous family for a month and fell in love. She was tender and delicate and initiated me into a pattern of love intricate and varied. I was delirious with happiness. There was someone to touch, to touch me, to laugh with, to tickle, to talk to in pidgin French, couchez avec me, cherie, to pretend with, to miss at night and to know she missed me. Her caressing fingers were like ferns, her full lips as soft as the petals of a flower, and her large sloe eyes like two lavender black skies. So of course at that very moment my father snatched my hand and yanked me away to go lay pipe and gaze smilelessly upon the natives of Lebanon, Jordan, Iran.

70

Then suddenly we were in the rubble and evil foul smell of Germany, first in Berlin and then in the Ruhr, in a small town with crooked streets and tiny gingerbread houses. Close by were the mines and the wood-rotted barracks which sheltered a few hundred seemingly forgotten prisoner-miners, Ukrainians. Lucky people—they could have been gassed and burned. Just miners they were, broad-boned men and women with no meat and no muscle. Hollow. Broad bones and sallow skin, in between nothing.

The war over a good year, they were free, and no one seemed to know what to do with them.

During the day they would leave the rotted barracks and congregate under a hot August sun in a large wire-enclosed courtyard, sitting on their haunches, standing and talking to one another, queuing up for food which American h.q. ladled out. I learned from some soldiers of the American division bivouacked in the town that in the first few days after being liberated many of the miners had become ill from their inability to ingest the richness of potatoes and meat, bread and butter, milk and eggs.

The mines had been flooded during the bombing raids a year before, at the war's close, and my father had been called upon to help pipe out the water. He was busy night and day, and I saw little of him.

Every day, lonely, I would saunter past the wire fencing and obliquely observe the miners in their ragged newfound freedom. They were free, and still in a cage.

Then one day an old locomotive hauling five cattle cars steamed into the freight siding. Nothing to do, no one to talk to, I went to watch some soldiers open the heavy doors, and when they did the stench which issued forth was as corrupt as all Germany.

"Some stink, eh, kid?" a soldier said just before he vomited. I urged my handkerchief on him, even though he didn't need it, so he would befriend me.

The five cattle cars were for the Ukrainian miners. The war won, they were free, they were at long last to return home. But when the commander of the division heard about the stench, he ordered the cars cleaned.

The trainmen, who were nationals of the eastern ally, just smiled and shrugged. A detachment of soldiers was given the job and as usual I went to watch them. Cow- and sheep dung isn't so bad out in the pasture or even in an open barn, but in locked cattle cars which have never been cleaned the dung hardens into cement and the stink sinks into the wood. But then there was another stench in the cars, the stench of human dung and something else. The smell of human death. The cars had not only the stink of all Germany in them, but of all the graveyards of the world.

The soldiers scraped, shoveled, hosed the cars down. I hated the stink, my eyes ran, but I couldn't leave, some indefinable perversity kept me close by. They worked hard and long; still the cars stunk. Big drums of lye were ordered by the commander in the gray-stone house overlooking the freight-yard siding. A phone call made, an order given, the drums delivered. Though I hated the smell of lye, for it recalled sharply to mind the green vomit smells of the hotel of my infancy, I forced myself to remain and observe the work. The men should have been issued gas masks, I thought, but of course did not mention it. My father had once beat me purple for giving advice for nothing.

At last the cars were as clean as they would ever be.

The following day I walked to the miners' courtyard

across the square of the freight-yard siding. I was going to wave farewell to the freed miners.

But the ex-prisoners sat on their haunches and refused to budge. Great consternation invaded h.q., in fact, the entire town. The freed miners had refused to budge.

The commander stormed. Hadn't he cleaned the cattle cars? What more did they want?

But in the wire enclosure the freed men and women sat silently on their haunches.

In the square between the cattle cars, which looked like wooden mastodons with open maws, and the barracks courtyard where the ex-prisoners sat, I stood with the others quietly. Overhead the telephone wires hummed in the breeze, as the gray-stone h.q. communicated with whomever it is that h.q. communicates with.

In our billet that night, as we prepared for bed, I asked my father about it, and he said, "They hate the tyrant who rules their country and are afraid to go home. So they have advised the commander they would rather clean latrines, do anything, but now they're free they don't wish to go home."

"They must be crazy," I said. "Everybody wants to go home. Me too."

"I, too," he corrected me coldly. "And be exact. Not everyone wants to go home. When a man is free he goes where he pleases." Even then, a boy not yet fourteen, I understood he was speaking for Taggart Strayhorn, who for his own reasons never wanted to go home, which of course meant I wasn't supposed to want to go home.

Yet I couldn't help but say, "There's nothing better than going home. To live in one place and make friends. You have to be real crazy—or have good reasons not to."

73

"Everyone has a different reason," he said in his cold manner. "To these men, home is degradation."

"What about us? Why don't we go home?"

"Because," he said sneeringly and for the thousandth time to be sure my very bones understood it, "home is where my wife and your mother was a prostitute."

I hated him and wished he would die and went to sleep wishing to be free of him. Because *he* was my degradation. The bastard, the no-good dirty bastard.

The next morning we heard that two of the miners had slipped out of their compound during the night and run away. Good for them, I thought, and even my father commended them.

After breakfast I strolled to the fence and saw that guards had been set at the gates. The miners stood about quietly speaking to one another. For many minutes I looked into the yard observing them. My impulse was to turn away—to run away, to say to hell with them, it was none of my damn business, why was I so interested in them?—yet somehow I couldn't. I felt a kinship with them and I wanted to be one of them.

I walked to the guard at the gate and asked him if I could go in. He said, "Sure," patting me on the head, himself lonely and homeless.

A friendly smile on my face, I strolled among the ragged, peaked lot. At the wire fence, on the inside looking out, sat a miner all by himself. I sat on my haunches next to him, smiled, offered a cigarette, stolen from my father's cache, held a light for him and lit one myself. We both sat there on our rears against the webbed fence, smoking and watching the sun like a growing flame rise into the sky. Neither of us spoke for neither knew the other's tongue. On occasion we stared at one another, each reading the mystery of the other's face, and smiled for communication. Wizened and hollowed from hunger, it was impossible to tell his age. For all I knew he was my contemporary. Except I had all my teeth; most of his were missing and his broad mouth in smile was a shiny red clay pit.

After lunch, I returned quickly, and we resumed where we'd left off, haunch to haunch, smile to smile, telegraphing our mysteries silently. When the August sun descended, I turned and reached out my hand. The ragged miner clasped it in his stub bony fingers and for a moment as we held one another's hand we recognized each other as brothers.

I saw the man was chilled now that the sun had gone; I raised my hand to indicate he must wait, wheeled, and left on the double. In a few minutes I returned, an old blue sweatshirt of my father's flung over my shoulder. I offered it to my friend, who took it and immediately put it on over his ragged shirt. Again we clasped hands, nodded, gazed at one another for a long moment, and I departed. I had a friend.

The following day, a colonel of the eastern ally appeared: broad-boned and white-pink skin; in between lots of meat and muscle. Standing in the middle of the enclosure, he spoke to his people quietly, yet with forcefulness. The freed men and women sat on their haunches, silent, and refused to move.

I stood in the square, my eyes on my friend, and had an urge to sing. Perhaps he and his compatriots would win.

In the strident shadows of late afternoon, the cattle cars with their doors wide open stood mammoth on the tracks. Overhead the telephone wires hummed between h.q. and out there somewhere.

After lunch, the sun a vivid white coal in the blue sky,

I ran to the fence. This time the guard said, "I'm sorry, kid, you can't go in."

"Aw, come on," I urged.

"No, you'll start an international incident."

I ran along the fence until I found my friend who waited for me. We smiled, the miner's red clay pit broad in friendship, its warmth ovening me. We sat side by side, touching through the wire. A guard, patroling the area, approached.

"Sorry, boy. You have to move on."

I tossed a bar of chocolate over the fence to my friend, we touched hands through the webbing, then I ambled off into the center of the square. There I sat, my back against a stanchion, and waved to my friend who now sat facing me.

The cattle cars stood huge, wide open and empty. In the compound the men and women lolled about speaking with one another.

I smiled confidently to myself. They looked tough and stubborn, perhaps they would win. Their bodies were hollow from years of slavery and hunger, but they had human hearts, two feet, not four; perhaps they'd win.

During the night, despite the guards, three more miners escaped. I half-hoped my friend was among them, but it turned out not to be so. In the gray-stone h.q. I could see the colonel of the eastern ally standing at the window, his jaw jutted, his eyes staring at the enclosure where his people sat on their haunches, refusing to budge. All day the telephone wires hummed and buzzed.

That afternoon, late, I timed my approach to the webbing when the guard's back was to me. I found my friend wearing the dark blue sweatshirt, gave him cigarettes, smiled, touched hands through the wire, then retired to sit at the stanchion in the center of the square. I pointed to the freight cars and shook my head, and my friend smiled his red clay smile and also shook his head no. A couple of tanks clanked past, a truck; then a company of infantry marched past, guns on shoulders.

I observed them as they marched across the square, did a column left, and filed through the gate into the barracks yard. The meaty colonel appeared from nowhere. Again he spoke to his people. They sat immobile. Silent.

I sat with them. Immobile. Silent.

The colonel turned to the infantry lieutenant, spoke quietly. The lieutenant called an order, his voice half-broken. The infantrymen fixed bayonets to rifles. Another order, and the soldiers fanned out, bayonets on the ready, about the courtyard.

I sat and watched my friend whose eyes never left mine. No, no, I shook my head; no, no, he shook his.

The colonel spoke to his people, his voice quiet but firm. The infantry surged forward slowly, their bayonets gleaming red from the twilight sun.

The freed prisoners sat, their sallow faces paste, biting their lips, then, as one, they slowly rose in defeat. My friend lowered his eyes.

"NO!" I shouted, my young voice ringing through the square.

My friend stood with the rest.

As they straggled in jagged column from the yard, the bayonets at their backs, many of them quietly wept. I with them.

In the square I stood stiffly, clenching my teeth, a young boy among men, my eyes following my friend in the dark blue sweatshirt.

They filed out, the bayonets behind them, and shambled slowly across the square toward the open cattle cars. My friend walked last, a shuffling, ragged figure, and when he passed me he lowered his head.

I stood facing the cars, my teeth clenched, my body stiff but my knees trembling, and my eyes followed the blue figure across the open, burning red square. As the men and women shuffled up the ramps into the cattle cars, I began to rock on the balls of my feet, my shoulders hunched and my hands half-fisted.

Smoke balled out of the locomotive stack, and as the first car and then the next were filled, a trainman slid the wide doors shut, locked the bolt into place.

Hesitantly the remaining men and women clattered into the fifth cattle car, my friend last. Before he entered, he turned his head to me and opened his hands, pleading forgiveness, but I hardened my heart and made no response. He dropped his shoulders in despair, swung around and was lost in the darkness of the cattle car. The door slid shut, the bolt clanked into place.

My fists closed hard, nails excavating flesh. Now all the soldiers towering above me with strained deliberateness faced about, their backs to the cattle cars, and stood at attention. Only I faced the balling locomotive.

Then in the stillness of the purplish-red square, just as the train began to roll, we heard a thump in the end cattle car. A thumping bang. Screams. Everyone in the square wheeled about. Another thumping bang, like wood on hollow bone. Many thumps. Louder. Faster. Thump, thump. Then squaash. Wild screams of pain.

All finally defeated by the iron wheels on rail.

I was sobbing, my heart felt it would split. Then, without consciousness or will, the skin on my face dry and tight, my heart thumping to the staccato beat of hollow bone on wood, I began to run, faster, faster, until each breath was a knife. Soon I left the mining town behind, heading west, into the sun, a dying coal.

A few weeks later, skin and bones, hollow, I was picked up at the border and returned to my father.

VIII

Alone, afraid, unpossessed, I returned that evening after
having left Madeleine Dearing to find Uncle Rob's roof
apartment atop an old, fine, and reputable hotel very
clean and airy. The smell must have become so bad they
had used a skeleton key to get in and scour it.

They had no right, I thought drearily, but accepted it.
Looked very Japanese, since it was austerely furnished,
for Rob's elegant twist of a wife believed less indicated
more.

The street's din down below sounded like the surf
heard from a great distance. What shark swam in those
waters? Every few minutes a jet whispered overhead.
The sun, down, sent up a fanlike fire, and the rivers like
molten iron ran out to sea.

Undressed; showered. The water was very hot and the
soap on my body sweet. The weight of my genitalia in
my hand was heavy and for a moment I felt tempted.
Began to think of the women I had known, the passionate
ones, the passive, the cold. Some had been beauties, those
not necessarily the most desirable. The most desirable
were those most secret.

Remembered Lillian and my body filled with desire.
She, like Rosalind when I first met her, had been a plain
girl with thin legs, only a slight curve to her hips and

smallish breasts. But she'd been secretive with me and that is what had made her most desirable.

"Who are you, Lillian?" I looked into her eyes, she withdrew them, turned inward. I touched her, she swayed in, then away, inward.

"I don't know myself," she answered, "so why do you ask?"

"Let's not be foolish," I said, "we're not seventeen, asking who am I."

She smiled enigmatically, and I became angry, thinking she was posing for *La Gioconda*. But no, she wasn't pretending, she was lost in the essence of where she turned in on herself. Isn't a woman a turning in on herself? Isn't a woman like a circumference—finite yet infinite? A man comes to an end, a dangle or a jut.

A woman says "Enter," and a man becomes lost in her endlessness. Like a young boy, I am enamoured of this secret curling, this turning inward, this twining. When I courted Lillian, every day I ran to meet her, wondering if that day I would discover her. We would eat what I had brought to her studio, a one-room affair shut off from the world by heavy black velvet drapes. It was over an undertaker's. We could smell the formaldehyde and incense through the cracks in the floor, and that lent greater secrecy to our meetings. Death was always present underneath us, smiling blankly and never answering any questions.

Lillian would be waiting for me enveloped in a red shroud of a gown, her long black hair piled high over her plain face, her almond-shaped eyes lowered so I couldn't see into them. We would eat hurriedly and then we would lie in her narrow hard bed in the blackened room and in order to find her thin body I would have to rummage about in her red shroud. When I entered her endlessness, she whimpered a faint "Oh," as if she were shocked and pained at my having found her and then her thin sinewy body would fling about with the strength of madness and then in a burning flash we would know each other. Afterwards she would cling to me, weeping silently—with pleasure or sadness?—at my having insisted that we apprehend one another.

Finally becalmed, she would rise from the bed, half draw the black drapes, remove the red gown to reveal her wiry sinuousness, turn on the record player and in the semi-darkness dance for me, her wiry nakedness in tight control as she formulated a discordant, fragmented choreography. And beneath us each day a new death, a clean corpse. As Lillian danced she would soon become again lost in herself, again become so secret I would not know her.

I would dress and leave her as she whirled, and within an hour, sitting in some off-beat Hamburg cave before a huge stein of dark beer, a record howling, the air damp and reeking of decay, I would become impatient for the next day so I could come running to seek her out, discover her anew.

Here I was soaping my body under a hot shower and there she was in her wiry infiniteness, her legs ever so slightly bowed awaiting me as if I were a mere parenthetical remark, when what I wanted most to be was an exclamation point. That is what I had been to Rosalind, who'd been just as plain, just as thin as Lillian, but with blond hair for black and round saucer-shaped blue eyes instead of sloe. And—and. . . . The water poured down on me, my eyes burned with soap, and there I was at exactly the place I wished most to avoid. To forget. And my head began to burst, overfilled with my present fraudulent existence, jammed full with that rotten, corrupt, oozing filth, that dog mess, that miasma of stink, that sewer of a memory which sought to invite romantic, innocent smiles in order better to hide the ever-present past. It was a memory which refilled itself as though it were Thor drinking Utgard-Loki's emptyless horn siphoning the polluted canals of my very own bowels. It decayed my will, sapped my strength, corroded the membranous tissue off the surface of my inner nostrils so that the mere smell of life made me howl with pain. I had right then and there to blank out the memory machine or I would choke the drain, plug the tub, and drown in my own dirty water.

The pain of remembrance sickened me, so to put a stop to one pain I sought another more immediate pain. I shut off the cold water of the shower and left on only the hot. I scalded myself until I screamed. My skin blistered. Only then did the old pain stop and the machine stall.

Somehow I was able to close the faucet and climb from the tub.

I dried myself, luxuriating in the excruciating hurt of rough towel on red sensitive skin. Brushed my hair in front of the mirror and admired my handsomeness. What a rogue!

The memory was gone. I was alive only at that moment. I poured powder on my blisters, then lay on the bed. How cool were the silken sheets, the symbol of my fiscal good fortune. When my mother died she left me one hundred twenty-five dollars; when my father died he left me five thousand dollars; when Barbara died in a plane crash with my child the insurance came to twenty-five thousand dollars and the out-of-court settlement to fifty thousand. Uncle Rob tripled the lot easily. Rob was a genius awaiting a Nobel prize. He could work brilliantly on his formulae, observe the Big Board with acuity, survey with an anxious eye his peripatetic wife, and whistle a Beethoven piano sonata simultaneously. A true Renaissance man.

How sweet to weep on silken sheets. During the lonely hours (I seek tears) when my father was off laying pipe, I used to daydream he would die and leave me his money. When Barbara began to bore me, I daydreamed her away too.

Who was next? Madeleine Dearing? Lots of dough cached away in that Grand Canyon of hers. I day-dreamed on my soft silken bed, in my roof shelter, my space station, of Madeleine. Wagered she was so big down there I could move in with a baby grand. What a concert we could play in that recital hall. If her breasts were suddenly to break their bonds the city would be devastated by the ensuing avalanche.

You're dying of grief, I said to myself.

Okay, then, let's shed a tear for the grievers. How happy we'll make them with our tears.

You're right—is there anything quite so sweet and joy-giving as the sight of tears shed for us?

"They water the lilies of our self-esteem," I said aloud with a histrionic quiver in my throat.

Brittle flowers.

Yeah, man, brittle. They endure even in the passionate desert of our tender sensibility.

What a gas. As tender as the curled tongue of a boiled shoe.

I began to feel better. What I needed was some normal, healthful activity. Get up and shake your ass. Visit some friends, have dinner, listen to talk of their children, of the war, of the slaughter on the throughways and parkways, of the sexual revolution, of the whatnot of daily existence.

Of our time.

There is no time like our time.

And what did they say in the streets when they heard the news report of the massacre in Agamemnon's flat 3500 years ago?

It's a symptom of the time.

So I slithered from my silken bed, chose a pair of soft yellow slacks, a powder blue shirt, and reddish tie. I was going out to see the world. But fortune was not with me. The phone rang. I knew at once who it was from the anxiety of the ring.

"Yes, Madeleine?" I asked, raising the phone to my ear. "Well, speak up." All she did was breathe. "Hurry up, Madeleine, or I'll hang up." She breathed faster, panted. I tried to calm her down, soften her. "Come, my sweet love, I've missed you. Have you missed me?" She breathed heavily, there was a tiny gurgle. I became enraged. "Talk to me! Talk to me, you goddamn fat whore. Talk to me!"

She gasped like someone sprawled on the beach catching his breath just having made it back to shore against the tide. "Say my name," I screamed at her, "my name, you fat cunt!"

A wet squealing sound writhed from the receiver into my ear like a snake, a little snake which coiled about the convolutions into my head. Then silence. I calmed myself, eased my own breathing. Waited.

She was making an effort; I could hear her panting, practically see her heavy breasts heaving with the labor of it.

Dumbstruck, I thought I heard her say, "David."

No, no, it had merely been my own hope that I had heard. Yes, I understood, she had become my hope—my last remaining hope. Then I heard my hope weeping, weeping uncontrollably, and she did move my heart and

I attempted to say a kind word, but none came. None. I was constipated with silence. Myself mute. And she wept, and shortly thereafter, just as I was beginning to glean enough energy from her tears to speak a soft word, I heard the click of her phone.

I finished dressing, though I realized I was going no place. I walked out on the roof, to its very edge, and stared down thirty stories to the street. I felt suddenly very serious, very squarish, very mature, as if I'd just come out of a smash-up to find myself safe and sound in my very own silk-sheeted bed.

There was a terrifying silence in my ears, my entire body in an exquisite repose.

I looked down the six hundred feet. It *was* a long way down. Bang. I wondered if concrete pulsated. I leaned far over the parapet and stared down, pointing like an arrow. I moved further down, then abruptly, cold and burning like a frozen foot, I stepped back and quickly sat down on the gravelly roof and vomited on myself. A terrible fatigue overtook me and I leaned back against the parapet to sleep under the sky like an upside-down bowl spilling out a vulgarly banging-pulsating universe on my head.

Later I crawled inside, and didn't venture out for a few days, neither to the roof nor the street.

Somewhere out there was Madeleine Dearing, Opera Star, who wanted what I couldn't give her and who had what I wanted and didn't have the guts to take. It wasn't a game I played with her even though I pretended it was. The pretension of a game was my form of muteness. And though I attempted to keep my mind a void, still the question wrote itself in a large nervous scrawl on my squeegeed slate: why did I refuse to be possessed and, subsequently, loved if that was exactly what I wanted? Why did I otherwise continually seek it out, sort of daring myself, teasing myself? Love would give me purpose. It was all as plain as the fat on Madeleine's ass.

What I wanted most, I feared most.

So I lived alone on Uncle Rob's rooftop. I didn't shave. I didn't wash. Took a cathartic to move my bowels. A radio alternately blasted rock or in a dulcet voice narrated the news of Harlem riots. Food was slipped through the door opened the length of its latch chain by a waiter. Bills were paid for me by check drawn by a slick chick in Rob's office. Minutes like sneaky, deceitful, carnivorous reptiles ate the days away so swiftly I never knew they existed. They? I! Madeleine I hid in some dark closet of my heart. I had affronted her enough.

Still, one breathes, eats, stores energy.

One morning, on rising, I cried, No, I'm a man, I jut, I dangle. I come to an end, and I refuse to have the end sneak up on me, devour me before I even know I'm alive.

Bounced about the flat on the balls of my feet, ripped a bloody breakfast steak apart with my teeth.

Beyond the roof I could see the city rolling under a haze of dirt, smoke, chaos. The town had the aspect of a volcano shaking itself down to explode but never doing so. Shooting blanks, so to speak. That's the city, isn't it? Always on the verge of insurrection, utter disaster, disorder, never quite accomplishing its purpose—or, at least, its desire. Filled with guilt and frustration, compressed violence sought exit from my every pore. With total lack of control, like a hubcap whipped loose from its whirling wheel, I swirled out and down into the subway, absolutely relishing every kick, crunch, and

87

pinch. Out I surged thirty minutes later into rampaging Harlem streets overflowing with black men, Afro-Americans all, shouting, punching, howling.

"Beat it, Charlie, you'll get yourself knifed," an old charcoal-colored man drawled in my ear, an old cadger escaped from a rundown Mississippi plantation. Toot'less, grinful, gray iron shavings for hair, his tobaccy spit cracking the pavement, he stood with me and the black crowd in front of the police precinct station yelling, stamping, cursing.

Shouting into his black grizzled ear, I said, "Not me, old man, nobody going to knife me, I'm blood, black as you are."

"Charlie," he said, "your skin's as pink as a boiled shrimp," which of course placed him more precisely geographically, for where would an old charcoal nigra know about shrimp if not from New Orleans?

Next to me, a tall broad-shouldered woman with red skin, a Cheyenne no doubt, was saying to her neighbor, a woman half her size with a creamy beige skin, "After my babies was born, all my organs was all growed together. The doctor told me I had a collapsible uterus. I ain't hardly got the stomach to talk about it now."

Her friend nodded sympathetically, then yelled at the top of her voice, "Love the bastards."

A trifle confused, thinking in Jap talk momentarily, since I was really in a foreign, exotic land, I said to my old friend, "Old Honorable Man, I'm as black as the tunnel from your rectum to your heart, yes I am, Hon. Old Black Man of New Orleans, begging your respectful pardon."

"Let us jive away from this boiling maze," Hon. O.B. whispered in my conchlike ear through his toot'less mouf.

"I got a little brown gal fo' yo' who'll suck you dry. Five bucks."

"Yo' dirty ole man," I cried above the din of a thousand gold-filled moufs screaming for the beauty of a hundred dead cops. "I don't want to sleep with your honorable daughter, I'se wanna free yo' all."

The Honorable Old Black became angry at my rejection of his black daughter and called out to the black men and women around us, all screaming, "KILL THE EFFIN' COPS," and he pipes, "Heah's one a doze white basitds who wanna free us. Le's string 'im up on a 'lectric pole. Letten us have a white lynch."

The screaming, shiny black, sweated crowd yelled in unison, "Heah! Heah!" so it sounded like a packed House of Lords, and four big black Afro-American bucks grabbed holt a me and raised me ovah deah haids lak ah wuz a side a beef and toted me tuh duh pole in an empty lot gardened with garbage. Everybody's yelling and stomping deah feet in jungle rhythms. Then one sweet voice, the leader, a big fat brown fox with a red wig and huge round blobbos protruding from her torn white blouse like liberty leading the people, she say, "Not hang 'im, eat 'im," and everybody howled with glee. Then she began to twist and shake her bosoms, and I was madly in love. Soon I'm bound tuh duh pole and I'm all surrounded and before me's a big black voodoo pot boiling over a fire and dey is all dancin' round me, the brown hard-butted girls with hard pointy dugs slapping at my privates publicly.

And I? Do you think I'm scared? There I am bound to the pole, stark naked, observing my future eaters through slitted eyes, an erection so hard one of the brown girls, a Eunice fox with long balloonlike breasts, in disgrace for some unknown acculturated reason beyond the experience of my Western mind, inpaled herself on its point, so that now thousands of sweating blacks are in a frenzy, dancing round me, singing hallelujah, hallelujah, clapping hallelujah, the big fat fox with the red wig singing the loudest and the sweetest, and de fire's gettin' hotter and hotter, and de pot she is boilin'. Soon I'se gonna be a cooked cock.

And I? I'm not scared, because I'm white and an optimist and I know I'm going to be rescued.

And rescued I was, believe it or not, by a committee of black gentlemen, the leaders of the Afro-American community, self-appointed. They saved my dirty white skin and nailed it to the wall with beautiful black love.

As they passed me gentle hand to gentle hand towards the subway station with the password, "He's blood," the black crowd sang;

> O Lord my God,
> When I in awesome wonder
> Consider all the worlds
> Thy hands hast made,
>
> I see the stars,
> I hear the rolling thunder,
> Thy power throughout the universe displayed.
>
> Then sings my soul, my God to Thee,
> How great Thou art.
> How great Thou art . . .
>
> Then sings my soul, my God to Thee,
> How great Thou art.
> How great Thou art . . .

All of which I swear did not happen to me as I gazed out over the city that hot afternoon when violence stalked the streets, the town like a volcano always threatening but never doing, just like an Italian movie.

In the evening, having come full circle, back where I had started, I stood at the window and stared across the roof to the city which lay under a black haze of grime, smoke, and night. Black though it was, I could see the North River broadly and regally commandeering the commerce of the world, and the East River running meanly, filthy with sewage—my hard-come-by leavings.

My violence spent, empty again.

To prevent myself from hurrying out to see Madeleine Dearing I went to a small café to eat the time away with Joe Hardman and a fashionable mod who for money did tricks. This girl was so constantly naked one barely noticed her sex. Food, she eschewed. Must keep the weight down, even at the breast, where to be in style she'd had the fat removed by surgery and replaced by that neat little device found on air mattresses. Every morning before slipping into her bra she reached for an air pump. We were eating—I ate, she nibbled—and drinking bourbon before leaving for my roof hideaway where, as she herself put it, I was going to stand her against the wall. From the adjoining booth we heard a fist slam the table and a man's voice blare, "Don't mention that cold soup of a second-rate genius to me. I crap on him. Crap! Being and nothingness. Crap!"

I became hysterical with laughter, for there in front of my eyes she sat, my little mod, a perfect replica of being and nothingness. I would take her to the roof and throw her a no-fuck.

Which was exactly as it turned out.

Yet I showed my back to Madeleine Dearing's very real, very substantial being.

Was the laugh on me?

91

By force of will I slowed the clock down. Rotted away in complete isolation in my roof apartment, seeing the universe spill out of that silly bowl like cold spaghetti and stale lumps of parmesan cheese. And in slowing it down, forced each minute into the mold of the minute before; still it moved at 3 g's (three times 32.2 feet per second per second, as Tag Strayhorn had taught me).

At last a cold steel chisel of energy pried its way in and I ventured out to the open roof without fear of plunging, and saw the stars.

The following morning when the room-service waiter slid my breakfast tray through the door, on it I found a thick packet addressed to me in an opulent yet hesitant hand. In the upper left-hand corner was printed in tiny, tidy letters, *Madeleine Dearing.*

A portentous gust set me quivering, and with fumbling hands I tore open the large wrinkled envelope and withdrew what seemed to be a morass of words, all written in the same full, stuttering hand, each word an obviously earthshaking effort. I could actually envision Madeleine sitting humped over her desk, her haunches overflowing the chair, her muteness cracking enough so she could eke out her hoarded operatic words, first hesitantly, then overwhelmingly. It was difficult to read, she struck out many words, crowded others in between the lines, and it was, I first thought, in complete maniacal disorder. Italian words with odd numbers attached to them followed by English words with even numbers, Italian and English words without numbers, all interwoven seemingly senselessly. But Madeleine, I knew, was no more insane than I. She was fat, she was mute, she lived strangely, as did I, but our malaise was precisely that no matter how mightily we strove for it we could *not* attain madness. What was apparent was Madeleine's anger at me, for she must have spent endless, arduous hours fragmenting, conceal-

92

ing, destroying the order of her thoughts merely to put me to the task of reconstructing them. Ah, yes, she was not easily to yield up her muteness to me. I'm sure as she so cunningly labored over her desk the thought must have occurred to her that I might very simply tear the whole mess to shreds. Still, she might have understood me better than I thought, have read me with her wise, probing, violet eyes and known I must, absolutely must, meet the challenge.

Thus crouched on a chair over the round oak table which Aunt Bry had brought over from Scotland in the hope it was King Arthur's and which she had placed near the large window to the roof terrace, I sweated to make order out of tortured chaos. For the first time in years I remained hard at work for endless hours, not once stopping to eat. By early next morning, using the numbers which she had spun out like thread through a maze as shrewdly constructed as that of Daedalus, I discovered a Monteverdi operatic monody, *Lamento D'Ariana,* its English translation, and a letter to me.

To gain the letter, I first had to unravel the Italian libretto and its translation, a part of which follows:

Lasciate mi morire.	Ah, leave me here to perish.
E che volete,	What comfort can you give,
che mi conforte in	what solace offer?
così dura sorte,	Love's martyr here I suffer,
in così gran martire.	bereft of all I cherish.
Lasciate mi morire!	Ah, leave me here to perish!
O Teseo, O Teseo mio.	O Theseus, O my love Theseus.
Si, si che mio	Yes, yes, I would tell
ti vo' dir che mio	thee now that mine
pur sei.	thou art still.
Teseo mio . . .	My love Theseus . . .

And then my reward.

Ay, David (she began),

I am lost. I called you, cruel David, so you could hear my very breath—my wretched heart. I cannot speak to you—I will not speak to you, for I am a wretched woman, huge and fat and I am lost, and yet—and yet I do daily pray that you will come to be entwined in my titian hair. Ay, David! how I hoped you would understand, you who are so cruel—and I so naked to your shafts, and you so fiercely cruel. I flew so high and have been brought so low.

Ay, David, if I could but speak the words which fill my heart but which my tongue, sad chained slave, cannot bear to utter, I know I could turn your cold cruelty. David, why do I write you? You have taunted me, demeaned me, have commanded me to speak. From whence shall I wrench the words? The empty cavern of my very self which I can never fill? Hungry I am, ay, David, wretched fat Madeleine. I am all flesh and mute and you are lean and starved—ay, what an exalted life we should have together. Do not command me to speak. *My heart is speaking; my tongue speaks not.*

What is it you know of me, David? What do you know of wretched Madeleine Dearing, Opera Star? I parody myself, for how else should I humble myself before my puritanical God? Do you know I was one of the great of the earth when I stood upon a stage with my opulent beauty and titian hair and sang? Even now I can move you, my cruel, cold lover, with but one four-measured note, Ariadne's cry; if thou couldst see, ah Heaven! if thou couldst see, ay me, how she is hungry, poor luckless Ariadne, by chance repentant, wouldst turn thy prow again and seek this island. My false-faced David, can you know when you ogle my enormous obesity that I was once very beautiful —sought after by many men? I married a man my elder by many years, a sophisticated, worldly man whom I dared to love and who nourished my beauty and innocence as Theseus Ariadne's thread, and he had no fear except for that which lay within the labyrinth of his own heart and I was one with him—yet he thought me innocent. Innocence! the most deceitful of all serpents, the conqueror even of immortals. No scandal ever touched us for I saw no one but my husband and my very own glory. We were arrogant in our love and knowledge of one another—and yet, yet, do you know there are many who live intimately together who know not one another—or themselves?

Thus, one morning a few weeks before we were to depart for Milano where I was to sing *Lucia* and vanquish the gods, as I sat before a window filled with golden sun, I turned to say goodbye to my husband, leaving for a few hours, and as he left for the very first time I noted gray in his lush beard and age in his body. He closed the door behind him, I shrugged it off, gazed out at a warm sun, enamoured of myself, lost in contentment. When of a sudden someone entered behind me and hovered about, someone agile of foot, silent, disdainful, his glance ice on my back. I whirled about, but whoever it was eluded me. Was gone. Nowhere in sight. Yet he laughed, scornful of me, much as *you* laugh, with a dark, harsh sneer and I knew—as I know with you—whoever it was meant to humble me. I had soared so high. So I went flying after him through the vast mysterious reaches of my innocent heart and he merely laughed, harshly, and was gone and I knew, ay, bitter David, I knew who had come to court me and disarm me.

And I knew henceforth he would never leave my side.

Lasciate mi morire, leave me here to perish. Speak! speak! in vain my weeping, in vain my crying for succour, wretched Madeleine. He would never leave my side. For it was unhappiness.

Dressed in a black silk Italian suit and soft fedora and white silk shirt and stone gray eyes with a harsh smooth face and a long thin taut body. Yes, unhappiness. Your twin, ay, David, false David.

And I would at that very moment have yielded up half my life and all my glory to have had the power to return to the minute before, but there is no returning, is there, David? *O Teseo mio.* Is it you who are Theseus or my husband, poor lost husband—which of you has left me on barbarous Naxos to perish, bereft of all I cherish? No, no, there is no returning, only muteness and the eternal filling of a bottomless pit. Ah, deaf as a serpent was I to his eyes' lamenting—storms, winds, hurricanes o'erwhelmed me. Oh, I am lost and no longer know whether I speak of him or me or you.

A few hours later my husband—a worthy word, a man husbands a woman and a woman houses

him, enwraps him in her wifely veil—soon after he
returned and before I could veil my eyes he saw
my unease and questioned it. I pleaded fatigue
and urged upon him the need for a journey after I
had made my conquest of La Scala.

O enough, David, for I know you will not answer, deaf you are for my heart is speaking, my
heart is speaking, yes, it is my poor tongue which
speaks not, and what speaks for you? I would tell
thee now that mine thou art, *O Teseo mio,* though
thou has left me, cruel, false David. If thou
couldst see how I am hungry, poor luckless Madeleine, what comfort could you give, what solace
offer? Can't you hear, O David? hunger speaks for
me and the voice is sorrow's.

Come to me, cold David, come to me and I will
house you in my wretched flesh and entwine you
in my titian hair.   Your mute Madeleine.

My mute, fat Madeleine.

I clutched at my clothes to dress, to fly to her, and at
the door I caught a glimpse of myself in the mirror, and
saw the harsh dark face of Taggart Strayhorn—and
sneered. A terrible chill sifted through my bones and I
trembled and quivered so I could hardly stand upright,
stumbled to my bed, and, freezing almost to death,
crouched under the blankets the entire day, wretched
Madeleine's letter clasped to my own hungering heart.

IX

Shattered by Madeleine's passionate cry, it took me a few days to recover, to grab hold of myself. First there was sorrow, then there was anger. False-faced David, indeed.

And who was gulling whom? Mute angel-face.

It appeared I had totally misjudged that overlarge, tongueless, sagacious, cynical, innocent lady of my evil dreams. Perhaps she wasn't so innocent after all. Perhaps *I* was the innocent.

Fury shook me as though I were a mangy whelp. I had enjoyed my despair, relished my salty tears, preened elegantly before the mirror of my agony; now she had come along to shatter my lean contentment with her lachrymose wail.

I must show the lady I was impervious to her wild cry—that I was truly cold, cruel David, with no intention of nourishing her hungry heart, I barely had enough to feed my own.

Thus, all puffed up with my shiny, brittle anger, I sat down at Bry's round oak table, and wrote:

> Dearing,
>   You're a fat fool if you think I will accept any words but those spoken with your tongue. Hearts don't speak, they merely pump hot blood. You re-

main mute, you say. Then stay mute for all I care.

Still, I must say, *cara mia,* my sweet little *cochon,* you are fullblown in my abdomen; yes, may He have mercy, every pound of you. Yet, despite your awesome roundness and softness, your florid, fluid flesh, you are excruciatingly sharp, my love.

Is it that which destroys me—that everything is exactly opposite to what it appears?

I understand completely why you love me. (Completely? A lie.) I understand—(Understand? Another lie.) I—(Still another.) You see, there's nothing left to say.

I know even if I were to devote all my remaining days to solving the mystery of understanding that I shall never understand.

My father, of whom I am but a thinned-out shade, and to whom all life was the precise measurement of the pipe through which the earth's steam and excreta flowed into the sea, would cringe at my doubt. But, of course, I rebel against my father. Why not?

I must admit I miss you, *O Fatso mio*—especially going with you to the concert hall and hearing you sing your four measures—four rungs to a heaven never reached.

I sigh, *cara mia,* my sweet little pig, and though I miss you I'll not come to you until I hear you say David with my very own ears. Only then will I know you recognize me.

I signed it with a big D followed by three kisses. Then I folded it very neatly, addressed an envelope, inserted the letter, and wet the gum of the flap with my tongue, an unnecessary detail since it was one of the new type which doesn't require wetting, but I wanted to send a bit of my physical substance to Madeleine. Next I called Uncle Rob's office down below to send up a messenger to hand-deliver the letter for me.

After he left with the missive, I was sorry I hadn't written in huge letters across each sheet, I. LOVE. YOU!

To avoid becoming mad with impatience for her reply, I decided I must find something to do, besides I was famished for the sight of people. Called the desk again to ask if Rob had returned with Bry. No, the nasal drip said, not for a couple of weeks yet. He was still off with his snake of a wife, that lovely girl who slithers, getting men to look and almost but not quite to touch, which keeps Rob in a constant state of anguish and desire. Too bad he's not returned, I said, and hung up.

An image of Madeleine squeezed into my narrow skull. No! Dress and get out of here.

Chose a neat pin stripe, a dark blue shirt with white collar, a darker blue chamois tie, and high-polished went down into the lobby of the hotel which pulsated with activity, if not life. Women were engaging men and vice versa. They were making out, connecting. I was being left far behind. In the Orinoco Bar a stoop-shouldered young Afro-American with a pure, clean, black skin was playing a cool modern jazz. At the bar I ordered a bourbon on the rocks. The predominant color was purple— the walls, the carpets, the skin tone of everyone present. One lady who suffered from jaundice was green as she drew delicate line drawings with her finger on the thigh of the elderly male baboon crouched alongside her. In the purple darkness I could see the small tables were filled with couples copulating with their eyes, though at some were trios, at a few, quartets.

At the crescent-shaped bar I stood between a business-like, controlled drunk and a man who resembled a ferret. The controlled drunk drank in a very precise manner, neatly, with intense concentration and dispatch, correctly. He raised his shot vertically with a pistonlike movement to the height of his mouth, then just as pistonlike horizontally to his mouth, at which point he opened his mouth and rammed the shot home. An efficient, well-organized man was he: conservative purple suit, purple white shirt, French cuffs, purple gold cuff links, purple tie, square face, purple even teeth, slicked purple hair. Neat. Him I ignored.

The man on the other side of me was searching for someone to talk to. His name I soon learned was Freddy, and he was in his fifties, skinny, with a long nose, sloping forehead, small eyes—Freddy the ferret with the friendly smile. All purple. I suppose I was purple, too, also disposed to friendliness, soft inside, yet sad, nourished by my lady's sorrow.

Freddy nursed his drink, what he wanted really was to talk. My bourbon on the rocks sparkled as I sipped at it. The beautifully black piano player played, the voices vied, the laughter loped, the ice melted. An excellent, warm, purple spirit invaded me. Madeleine would answer my letter, concede to my request, recognize me, and my life would accelerate, whirl. Freddy the friendly ferret smiled and I returned it with one of my specials—all teeth and twinkling eye.

"Ah, women," he said at last. Very unusual topic, I mused to myself.

Aloud I said, "Nothing like them."

He laughed as though I'd said something extraordinarily witty, and I joined him—perhaps I had. "Every one of them is different," he said. A great truth.

"Yes," I shrugged, sipping bourbon, "except when you hold them upside down they all have a mouth and a beard."

Freddy really roared at that one, and I again joined him, very pleased with myself. He was juiced. I was becoming purpler by the second. On the other side of me the businesslike drinker drilled away.

Encouraged, Freddy said, "They're very difficult, though," and I smiled him on. "I have one of those new ones," he continued, "who takes me back to when I was a boy. She's got old-fashioned kewpie-doll lips, very long black lashes, a chopped-up haircut, long legs, a small round ass, no waist, and little delinquent breasts—you know, the kind that sag, with long black nipples which look like those Dutch cigarillos the *mafiosi* have taken to smoking." Ha ha, I laughed to myself, this old pukka sahib's right on the hookah. "This friend of mine," he resumed, "is a red-hot number out of the past, even though she's only twenty-four. Good age for you," he said patronizingly.

"Too young for me," I said. "Like them mature, when they can appreciate a young man." If he was going to pull age on me, he would have to take it both ways. He looked at me as if I'd just made him out to be the oldest man in the world. To make it up to him, I said, "I hope I look as well as you do when I reach your age," which of course only made it worse. I thought poor old Freddy was going to cry, but he took a sip of his drink and caught hold of himself. He really wanted to tell his story.

"As I say," he resumed, "she's out of the past—or maybe it's just that it takes thirty, forty years for the world to

102

turn full circle. Hell, flappers would feel right at home these days, except they'd be on LSD instead of hootch."

I agreed. "Yeah, the way they look reminds me of pictures I have in my mother's old trunk." We both sipped, moving our drinks along, past recollection refreshed.

"This friend of mine," he said, "frugs instead of blackbottoms, that's all; and makes big black shifty eyes at all the men—even me, though I'm not so hot and can only get it up about twice a month. She's been putting me on for a couple of years—and taking me off. A very hip little cat who knows every grind and wind on the road."

"One of the terrorists of the sex revolution," I interjected, feeling very bright.

He observed me with renewed interest. "Yes, the counterrevolution will soon begin." Now his little purple rodent eyes gazed into the future, and I was certain he envisioned a circular guillotine where all alleged reactionary dogs would be beheaded in a forced circle jerk. But only for a moment. I wanted him to continue his story, so I said, "Well, what modern man wouldn't like a hip kid who frugs instead of blackbottoms?"

That started him off again. "She's got a husband and I have—or had—a wife who stopped wanting it a year after we were married." I nodded in full understanding, empathising with him, since hadn't I been married to a girl named Barbara? "One night," he said, "I picked up my little frug a block or two from her house—supposedly she'd stepped out to buy a loaf of bread—and accelerated to a dark street which had few houses but lots of bushes and trees and a dead end. I just had time to park and push the light button in before the little nymph began putting me on—in her hurry she ripped skin with my zipper. The next thing I know someone's blinding me with a flashlight. She bit down so hard I thought I'd lost it forever. Was months ago and I still wake up screaming. Well, it was a private dick working for my wife. So I agreed to give her a divorce and made ready to bargain strenuously on alimony, knowing no one in the whole world would want to marry her and I'd be stuck for life. To my surprise she said she didn't want alimony, she wanted cash. Happily I sold my house, my car, cashed in my bonds, and gave her thirty-five thousand dollars, all I owned." Freddy emptied his shot, and to keep him company I did likewise. On the other side of me, vertical, horizontal, ram! "A day after the Mexican divorce," Freddy said, "she married my neighbor and I discovered they'd been lovers for fifteen years. Every Wednesday morning, five minutes after I'd leave the house he'd show up. Ate my food, drank my liquor, laid my wife, used my garden tools. She'd just been waiting to clobber me." He twitched his snout and tears glazed his eyes. Hardly the man, I thought, to tell my own tale of woe to, a weeper, usually the cruelest kind.

Sure enough, now that he'd unburdened himself on me, filled me with his sordid little memoir, given me his load to carry, he paid for his drink, wrinkled his snout swiftly a few times ferret-fashion and scurried away, his skinny tail lost in his droopy trousers.

Now I felt worse than when I had entered the Orinoco Bar. I hate to drink alone. On the other side of me the drinking machine was going at it with perfect timing, the pistons well oiled, a truly great purple machine. In the semi-darkness of the café over the gentle river sound of whisky sipping and sibilant whispering could be heard the brazen screech of purple cormorant and orange Venezuelan parrot, my glassy-eyed brothers and sisters of the natural world. How I envied them: they all looked so happy, totally free. Remembered something Burke had written, to the effect that anarchy was not freedom, it was enslavement. Wasn't I a slave? But I didn't have a chance to think further about it because my pistonlike barfly tapped me on the shoulder.

Face to face, I saw he appeared surly. "Yes?" I said, smiling, not wishing to tangle with that machine just yet.

He batted a purple wink which I fielded on one hop and returned on a line.

"Know why I drink?"

Here was a story I didn't want to hear, but I wasn't looking for a fight, so I went along. "Why?"

"Because I like it!" Whereupon, machinelike, neatly, he bowed and, as I applauded, departed.

With a regal bourbon salute to my fellow drinkers and revolutionists I also left the Orinoco.

I was happy.

The wind gusted dust into my eyes, my ears became gritty, my snot black with grime.

Still I was happy.

Why? Who knew and who cared?

I was happy.

The wind blew the girl's skirts thighward, and I was excited at the sight of the kite. There, across the street, was a building whose lines I admired. Stopped to stare and was happy with its height. Though a box, it had color and mystery.

Sat on the curb and though people sneered I didn't care and was happy. Madeleine, O Madeleine *mia!*

Rushed, coattails flying, through the streets. Flew, flew, towards her house. I would stand in the little cement court below the pavement level and sneak a look into her place, my eyes like mice searching out some crumbs.

How strange. Met the blind man with the flesh eyes and his dog, but he was morose and wouldn't speak to me. "Go away, mister." He hurried along, playing his harmonica, "Melancholy Baby," pulled by his skinny hound.

I shrugged and increased my pace so I passed him, restraining a desire to steal a coin from his dog's back. Through the blustery dark streets I sped ecstatically to Madeleine Dearing's and soon found myself at my old stand in the corner and like a soldier who's been taught how to look around a tree without showing too much head to the enemy I sneaked a look through the window.

The bullet that hits you, I once read, is the one you don't hear. That was the way it had been with Madeleine and myself. I'd begun by playing a game with her—I was the hunter and she the rhino on our own bleak African plain. Would I have dared take on a strong healthy beast? No, not me. I had dared all on this failing rhino. And somewhere along the hot dusty *manche* the wounded beast had turned and, gathering her last remaining strength, smashed me down.

As I peeked through her window I realized I'd been smashed down hard and though now the wound was numb soon the numbness would vanish, the pain would begin, and the gash to fester and fever.

My great love sat on the piano bench, dripping over its edges, her arms on the keyboard, her head on her arms. Was she sleeping in this silly fashion? Her hair—ay, David, entwine you in my titian hair—looked like a barn sparrow's nest; her black shapeless house gown covered her like a sack, but hiked up at the knee to reveal her fat doughy thighs. What a beaut!

Overcome, I knuckled the window and saw her quiver

—was it fright or a subterranean knowledge that it was David Strayhorn? Slowly her head swiveled towards the window. Lying there, her eyes stared sideways, chinky slinky, into mine. What was it I read in her eyes as she recognized me? Love? Fear? Hatred? Desire? All. Yes, desire, too. She hungered for me. What an astounding feeling overcame me at the thought that she hungered for *me*. Captured by an ocean ebbtide, my strength was puny against its indomitable will. Yet, I also felt myself grow hard, stub. I wished to bury myself in her huge softness, my end to become lost in her endlessness. Everything about me turned upward, reaching. Fool, I spoke to myself, you think there are stars up there. Only coal shined up on the seat of His pants. Stars—stars are for children. I could see Madeleine's violet eyes soften, widen, open, spread as her tongue moistened her lips which like mine had become thick with desire.

Then she leaped—*she* leaped—and ran from the room, and then I saw her at the iron-barred door. I plunged towards her. We pressed to one another and I could feel her soft warmth touch me through the bars.

We kissed, our hands sought and found and clasped. Soon the bars would melt between us.

But she unclasped me and stepped back. I waited, hopefully. At last, at last. Yet, though her cheeks were wet with tears, I saw her face harden with hatred. Before the inner wood door slammed in my face I spat in her eyes.

Lost in the gray night, I shuffled homeward.

X

Lasciate mi morire. Leave me here to perish.

My eyes were so dry every time I blinked it felt like sandpaper on my cornea. I sat in the darkness, staring excruciatingly into the night which concealed the city below. Madeleine had chosen for herself the role of Ariadne, doomed to weep on her cruel barbarous isle. And I? I was not Theseus, I had no great city to rule. Must I, like my father before me, just wander, to die sneering in some strange land?

I hated him for the mark he had put upon me. But hated him most for what he had done after I met Rosalind. That had been my chance, and I had lost it. Now I was like him, and I despised him for it.

Rosalind, Yes, O Rosalind, my love. My sweet little bird.

We remained a few miserable years in Germany, then went to England where my father had contracted to be a consulting engineer to the authorities rebuilding London and Coventry.

I was seventeen and always alone, dressed to kill and murder in my eyes for the ladies. I was a full-grown man and no one took me for a child. Tag was always busy and I was on the town.

Saw her standing alone in the middle of Piccadilly Circus going no place, killing time. She had a sharp, pointed nose, saucered blue eyes, gawky legs, and her thighs formed a curved furrow under the thin dress. She wasn't a very good-looking girl and the white-faced, austerity-fed boys swirling about her couldn't see her at all. Hungry, they wanted someone with more meat on her.

I didn't know why, I merely walked over and said, "Hello, I'm not going anyplace either."

And she responded with a shy smile, and I abruptly became shy myself. After introducing ourselves, we didn't have much to say to one another; she was very shy and I, at that time, lost my tongue when confronted by a girl who was as the soldiers used to say legit. A man could talk to a fox or a pro because he knew without thinking she was here today and gone tomorrow. But with a girl who was legit it became a serious matter, a project, an undertaking. And she was very legit I could see immediately with my worldly-wise seventeen-year-old eyes—good times, having a gas, wasn't her entire program. She wanted a fellow but didn't have the upsuck know-how, didn't even want him to spend his money foolishly. Taggart Strayhorn was no miser, and I always had more than enough in my wallet.

She was too conscious of not being good-looking. But she had, I thought, a nice face—just a trifle too pointy, that's all. Those big round blue eyes were kind, yet sad, as if life hadn't been too friendly, much like mine, and there was one thing she had I really liked very much— big buck teeth, white and strong, so I found her smile charming, though, again, sad-edged.

We hardly spoke the first night we dated, and we danced poorly in each other's arms, she blaming herself and I myself. This sad-edged girl twinged my heart. But somehow we laughed here and there and I walked her to her flat in Chelsea, near the river, in the darkness and the wet air. We shook hands—she was painfully correct—after having made a date to meet again the next night at the club where we had danced.

When I walked into the club—a trifle late—she was already there, greeting me with a big toothy smile. Though my heart fell a mite when I saw her pointed face, still I felt attracted to her big white buck teeth and those round blue eyes, kind, yet with an undercoat of defeat. I realized since there was nothing else attractive about her I was forcing myself to discern something that was. Yet, well, buck teeth *were* attractive, fetish or no.

As we shook hands our shyness asserted itself and we sat quietly and uneasily drinking 'arf 'n 'arf. We danced a bit, becoming less clumsy, and I tried joking. "I'll soon be good enough to teach in a dancing school."

She smiled apologetically and opened her mouth to say something, and I knew she was about to denigrate her own talent, so I interjected, "You dance well," but this obvious lie only made her stumble and then she blushed and I regretted I'd opened my idiot mouth.

We didn't speak for a half hour, but without thinking we held hands very tightly even when we weren't dancing, until I noticed the sticky sweat and my constipated fastidiousness asserted itself and I let go. We drank lots of ale, sat silently, danced. Though she laughed merrily, those giant teeth sparkling, when a cockney music hall comedian machine-gunned jokes which went right past me as though he'd spoken in a foreign tongue, and I found myself admiring those teeth more and more, having fantasies about them. O, no, I thought, she's a good girl.

Again I walked her home in the late night. As soon as we were out of the crowd I observed her relax as if the fact she wasn't good-looking weren't too important. And I liked her better for it. This time when we passed the Tate Gallery we stopped, went back and sat on the steps though it was cold-wet as it gets in London even in July. We smoked, held hands, and exchanged exhortations on what a grand time we were having together. We wanted more than we were giving one another, so now we were making it up.

Cigarettes burned down to their ends, we resumed our stroll to her flat. We made a date to meet again soon, shook hands, but neither wished to let go. I kissed her, her mouth tasted sweet, pressing my lips hard against her teeth; I liked the hard feel of them and wanted to run my tongue over their surface, but held back and let her go. She seemed to wait for me to try again, but I thought better of it and said goodnight.

Liked her very much, her sweetness and sadness and shyness touched something deep in me, but I was raunchy, too, and wanted to satisfy my urge. Quickly I walked back to Piccadilly and soon, of course, a soft clutching hand like a poltergeist from the shadows grabbed at my elbow. Once in the pro's chilly, wet room, under the weakly lit lamp, and I saw the ghost herself, tired yellow dough, I couldn't do it, just petered out. Disgusted, I paid her and left, the woman's cracked contralto insults trailing after me, because, as I well know, even a pro has pride.

Rosalind and I were less shy, more talkative, the following night, and we left the club early. I'd made up my mind before going to meet her that even a good girl wants loving and why not? Once in the dark streets, our fingers linked, we stopped speaking. I had seen by the way her eyes shone that she was overwhelmed by her feeling for me and somewhat astounded, too, by my constant attentions. She was a strange girl, really. Gentle and sad and someone for whom on first sight one felt compassion, yet when we were alone she wasn't quite that way at all. She stood firmly on her own two feet, didn't agree with everything I said, was cheery and ribald. She was alive, damn it, and I didn't have to feel compassion for her at all.

As we ambled through the streets of old London, a very permanent city, we stopped every few feet to kiss in the dark, each kiss more urgent, and her sweetness took my breath away. We kissed and held on tightly, words a dismissed surplus, our lips and straining bodies speaking with all the meanings. Kissing and hugging and walking and not talking we managed to reach her flat, a shabby rundown tiny two rooms.

There we spoke with a wordless urgency.

Afterwards I realized how really soft a skinny girl could be. Bony and pointy all over, no, she wasn't a very handsome girl, yet the mesmerizations of love made her soft, and my God how the sweet sadness tore at me.

We drank tea from cups mended with glue, her poverty appalling. We spiked the tea with kisses, our lips bruised but who caring. And as we sipped the hot tea and munched biscuits, we stared long into one another's eyes. I had expected her to be ashamed, but no, her eyes shone and the flush dimmed the pointiness of her features. She hadn't been a virgin, and I was slightly surprised, but of course it didn't bother me, and who cared since I could see she wanted more of that wordless speaking. At seventeen the well never runs dry.

"You are the dearest person I've ever known," she told me softly the next morning after I said goodbye at the entrance to the office building in which she worked as a secretary.

Brought up by Taggart Strayhorn, all I could manage

was, "I like you very much," when what I wanted was to take her in my arms and tell her she was the most beautiful girl in the world. I stood watching her as she entered the door, a gangling skinny girl with very blue eyes and a pointed nose.

My father never asked, and I never told him. We would see each other for breakfast on occasion, he would ask if I needed any money, give me a wad before I even answered, and be gone. Free as a bird I was and saw Rosalind every day, though I was afraid of her feelings for me and mine for her; I believed they could only lead to disaster.

Though I told her little about myself, she was no miser and told me all. She'd lost two brothers with Montgomery in Africa, her two sisters were at home in Nottingham with her mother and father, who worked on a machine lathe. She had never been in love before though she'd had an affair three years before, when she was eighteen, "And how old are you, by the way?"

"Twenty-two," I lied smoothly; opposed to her innocence, I felt like forty-two.

"I thought something was wrong with me because no boy ever tried to make love to me. When this boy asked I thought I should, and I did. It didn't last long because I didn't love him and he didn't love me—we just needed to find out about ourselves. I've always hated myself for not being pretty, and once thought of cutting the tip of my nose off, and yet I know I'll be able to give you all the love you want. I love you and I don't care if you don't love me."

"You're lying," I said coldly. "You have to care. You HAVE to care," I suddenly screamed, revealing my temper, and immediately thereafter my tears.

She merely stood there in her shabby flat staring at me,

her eyes round and porcelain blue and her nose twitching like a rabbit's, so I despised myself and hated her.

After a few moments of silence, I said, "I do love you."

She looked very hard at me, no fool, and quietly said, "Don't lie. I know you don't but you want to."

"Yes," I answered, her sad edge cutting through the ice of me. "I want to. I want to. And maybe I will." Right then I would have given my life to love her. "I'll try hard, as hard as I can." And she kissed me, biting my lip with her teeth.

"Perhaps you'll tell me some day and I'll understand," she whispered softly. "But I am so utterly happy loving you that I don't care. I have so much love to give you and I'll give it whether you love me or not. Do you know why? Because no one has ever been so kind as you—as considerate." Was she speaking of me? "And because I'm happy loving you," she continued softly, so softly I hardly heard her. "Terribly happy. Is it indecent loving you so quickly, having slept with you so quickly? Since the war it seems everything moves more rapidly, everyone loves rapidly—is it because the war gave us all a terrible fear that the world will soon end and we must hurry to get all our lives in? Don't be reticent with me, tell me all there is to know about yourself, I won't ever hurt you with what you tell me. I love you."

And I felt like a thief, for I took as much as she could give and gave little back.

But I did see her as often as I could get away, which was nearly always, since Taggart Strayhorn was continually off laying pipe and his fancy ladies. Yes, that great big hulking puritan. I don't think he ever went with a legit in his life, including my mother.

But I did, I had Rosalind, whom I tried to love, tried

to give as much as she gave me, but found it impossible to squeeze anything like love out of my guts. I consoled myself with the thought it is impossible to manufacture love. She understood and I was amazed how much understanding there was to be found in love. And pain.

In bed she was gentle as opposed to my hungry fierceness, but I came to know her in the way my father's Bible said, and learned to give her pleasure. I couldn't give her love, the least I could give her was that. It took great patience and restraint, but I learned.

In the fall of the year, about four months after my having met Rosalind, my father's work approached an end, but I paid no heed to the warnings. For only Rosalind and her love filled my mind.

Then one Sunday morning, standing coldly before me, he said, "Be ready at six. India." Curt, just like that—couldn't spare the words. "And don't try what you did in Germany. You're still a minor."

"You don't have to remind me," I said; began to say something particularly nasty but thought better of it. Tried another tack. "Why don't you send me to school here—you've often promised? I'll take an engineering course and then we can work together." I hoped he would listen. Rosalind was waiting for me in her flat.

He looked at me not unkindly, and suddenly I had hope. "No, not here, the English are terrible engineers." Just another excuse. He held on to me so tightly one would have thought he loved me.

As soon as he left, I dressed and ran all the way to Chelsea, to Rosalind's flat. When I panted in, she was standing at the cooker, her hair in disarray, her pointy nose shiny. When she saw me, she just stood very awkwardly, her hands full of whatever she was preparing for us—like children, we played house!—her long skinny legs bare and slightly curved and her toes showing in the fancy mules I had bought for her. We stared at one another shyly for a moment; she began to cry, for she had read in my face the message I'd brought. The marvelous earthfed love she had for me would soon be lavished on a void.

I let her cry as I put on the hot-water heater, cleaned the flat for her. She merely sat on a chair weeping, turned in on herself so that her bony shoulder blades protruded from her back like vestigial wings. My bony malnourished angel, I thought. When I finished cleaning, turning down the flame on the cooker, I picked her up in my arms and placed her on the bed. I undressed her, bathed her, dried her in a big Turkish towel, powdered her. Then I sat her up. She had stopped crying, merely stared at me with her sad little smile, and I brushed her hair, a fine yellow silk, stopping now and then to kiss her lips or her ears or her small breasts, she sitting there permissively, sniffling just the tiniest bit, her blue eyes shining with the wetness.

With almost maniacal strength I enfolded her in my arms and we made love without any preliminaries and she was as urgently fierce and cruel as I had ever been, and then she had to jump up with a cry because the food on the cooker had begun to burn and smoke.

As we ate, we said no more than a dozen words.

The clock hands urged me to go. As I approached the door, she gave me a red sweater she had knitted for me, and her smile made the pointy nose classic, her legs appeared straight and rounded where they weren't. We kissed quickly and I backed out of her suddenly limp arms.

She cried out, "DAVID!" and I couldn't even turn around and say, "I love you." What sense was there to it?

It was when we were fully packed and ready to leave the hotel that I understood I loved her and couldn't bear to leave and never see her again. O Rosalind, my love.

Abruptly I stood before him, almost his height but half his breadth. He was a powerful man, who dressed casually, almost sloppily, an engineer who loved nothing more than to work on the job site, knee-deep in muck. I knew he deplored my penchant for elegance, and perhaps that is precisely why I enhanced it. Besides, I knew it made him wonder, though never out loud, about my virility. He need not have wondered, I was his son. We were a matched pair of studs—gene for gene, our fingerprints almost identical.

Dark and harsh, his black eyebrows raised quizzically, he faced me, waiting for my words.

"I'm not going," I said quietly. "I'm going to stay here and get married. I have a girl." Sort of half-expected him to laugh in my face, except, of course, he never laughed.

Instead he sneered, the bastard, turning impatiently back to the valises. "You're only seventeen—you're coming with me. Get moving."

No, you're not turning away from me this time, I thought, my sweet skinny bird fluttering her wings in my heart. Gathering together all the courage I was ever to possess, I repeated, "I'm not going. Ever. I love Rosalind. She loves me. You don't. Never have. And you don't need me and I don't need you. Even your lousy money. I'll earn my own. Despite yourself, you've taught me to be a free man, I'll be one to the day I die. I'll not go with you. Never. I love Rosalind. For once in my life I love someone and she loves me and we'll have a home and I'll not leave it for the rest of my life."

He looked at me now, yes, he did, his dark face suddenly plaster white. For a strange moment I had the feeling he was afraid of me or of his violent feeling about me, whatever. "You don't need *me?*" he cried.

"No, I don't need you," I shouted, holding his eyes which seemed to squirt away. Yes, he was afraid of me and I felt a terrible power. I could be free of him.

"And I don't need you?" he asked, forcibly restraining his emotions, softening his voice.

"No, you don't need me. You never have. You don't need anybody. Just yourself. She told me, Mama did, how you left as soon as I was born. She told me I was yours. Well, maybe I'm not." I'd said it at last. It had lain between us all the years of our life. Life? A poor excuse of an existence.

That really hit him. He raised himself to his full height, I could see all that strength and all that pent-up hatred and I knew at last since I had gotten it out now he would. But not with words. That was too difficult for him—to say it out loud for all the world to hear. That was where his fear lay, of course, that some day it would be said and then he would have to kill me. He just raised his huge fists and clubbed me hard. I fought him back with my nails, my knees, my teeth. He was wild with it, the fear and the hatred and the sorrow of it. He beat me till I was limp, broken, smashing my face—his face it was, Taggart Strayhorn's, and the blood was Polly's. And as he beat me till I was blind and almost deaf, smashed, from behind his clenched teeth, almost like the screech of a wounded hawk, he kept repeating, "I don't need you? I don't love you? You are my son. Am I to be left alone?"

XI

Lasciate mi morire! What comfort can you give, what solace offer?

Through the entire night, my eyes blinking with pain as if sandpapered, I stared excruciatingly into nothing. Madeleine and I were doomed to keep slamming doors into each other's face. Yet, I remembered just before her face had hardened with hatred, before the wood door had slammed in my face and I spat in her eyes, her cheeks had been wet with tears. What had intervened? What?

As if in answer to my question, the room service waiter knocked on my door. And again there was a letter from Madeleine Dearing. No labyrinth, no code, no puzzle—just a letter in her opulent, operatic hand.

> David Strayhorn,
>
> What is it you desire from me? Why have you sought me out? Why have you asked me to reveal my heart? Merely to demean me with your filth and detestable arrogance, to trick me into your own private intimate hell? Your false, fake face, you cruel wretched man, what does it conceal? What crime have you perpetrated on what defenceless creatures? Ay, David, you are despicable

in your vileness. My husband left me, food for
wild creatures, food for the pitiless and fierce wild
creatures, left my bones to be scattered, for such
as you. Who are you, cruel man, to call Madeleine
Dearing *cara mia?* What is it you are insinuating?
I am lost, bereft, naked, revealed to you in all my
obesity. You offer me your arms only to lead me to
hell. You are of clay, but I was once an immortal.
Haven't you harmed me enough, cold David?
Must you call Madeleine Dearing *whore?* *Cara
mia . . . cara mia.* No, I will never speak your
name, for one such as you I will never break my
vow to remain mute. . . .

On and on she raged, so far as I could understand, inco-
herently. She was expending her entire wrath on me because I had dared call her *cara mia,* which even in my ig-
norance I knew merely meant *my dear.* She threatened to
have me arrested if I did not stop molesting her. Then
with a suddenness the storm ceased, the waters became
calm, and very simply she wrote:

David, I have begun to dream. Does that portend
that I have begun again to live? Last night I
dreamt I was in a ship's cabin with my husband.
We stood at the open porthole and gazed out at a
shimmering golden sea. We kissed, caressed one
another, made love, were happy, gay. As I lay on
the bed, he rose to leave me, smiling secretly, enigmatically. He said he would soon return. As he
left, he locked the door from the outside, to protect me, he called out. I lay on the bed observing
the sea shimmer on the ceiling above me. As I
mused, the ship began to pitch and roll, sea spray
splashing through the open porthole. I tried to rise

from the bed to close the window, but I was unable to leave the bed, as if I were bound. I heard my husband outside the door, and I called to him, told him to hurry. But he did not open the door. And the sea began to pour into the cabin, a great gush of sea, and I could not rise and my husband would not open the door. I heard myself singing Ariadne's lament, Ah, but he does not answer; ah, deaf as serpent he to my lamenting; O storms, O winds, O hurricanes o'erwhelm me and I drown beneath the sea. Still my husband did not answer and soon in my dream I saw myself floating face down. . . .

She concluded her letter with a tenderness, with a cry, "David!"

That was all.

I believed she had become completely deranged. Went to groan on the pot; hands pressing against the walls to help, sweating and cursing, nothing moved. I became euphoric with pain, self-righteous with pain. Yes, I thought, there's nothing like pain self-inflicted to give one authority over all those without.

As I drank my tepid coffee and ate my sodden toast and thought of Madeleine, I became frightened. Who needed that ton of trouble? Enough. I decided to stop seeing Madeleine, to stop hounding her, to try, hard as it would be, to stop thinking of her.

Arrivederlá, cara mia. Goodbye, my dear.

XII

As soon as I decided to stop chasing after Madeleine Dearing, to give up my insane dream of the exploration and conquest of that vast, unknown continent, the stone in my belly plummeted, my bottom fell out, and I was left with a jagged hole and an emptiness.

Just as it had been when Barbara was alive.

Three years after I left Rosalind and London, just before I reached my adulthood, my father died, tragically enough, while he and I were doing field work in Cooch Behar, where he'd come to solve a sewage problem in order to prevent an epidemic of cholera.

I had him burnt to ash, collected what money the Indian government owed us for the pipe laying, shook the lady Coochers out of my black hair, and hopped the first plane for the States five thousand dollars richer than I'd been the day before. Gave it to Uncle Rob, now married to the lascivious Irish girl, Bry, a charitable lass who couldn't deny herself to any male between nine and ninety. Even to me one night while Uncle Rob nervously paced the floor of his lab awaiting the birth of a new batch of bugs. Rob couldn't manage Bry, but he managed my money so well it reproduced nest eggs faster than a white pullet.

An orphan now, the sundry Strayhorns around the

country pitied me. I permitted them the pleasure, a wan smile etched on my brooding face. Inwardly, I crowed: I was a free man. Though even then I found it necessary on occasion to hide in dark corners in a black funk. But I was a tall, slender youth with money in the bank, a dark handsome face, and my future ahead of me. I wanted a home and a wife, sick to death of the wandering. I would have been happy to send for Rosalind, but she had long since married.

Uncle Rob obtained employment for me as an IBM systems machine operator with a large credit company, a subsidiary holding in Robert Strayhorn's vast empire, related of course to his scientific work. In addition to being a biochemist, he was also a mathematician and a perennial Fund snatcher.

Since I was competent, 311-08-984-7 could 999 times out of 1000 be found cohabiting the correct slot with 311-08-984-6. The 311s were specials, those anal characters who paid promptly regularly. The 309s were the mean average normals, slow pay but rarely delinquent beyond the grace period.

The salary was $7500. I had four girls under me who came at staggered times. Vacations, pension fund, welfare fund, and I could think any damn thing I pleased while slotting 413-836-023-1-X belly to belly with 413-836-023-2-X. 413s were the *nouveaux riches*. This sequence was a little tricky, unsure, since too much wealth too quickly earned leads to wild deformation of life pattern in reality situations resulting in sluggish feedback. But after a time even the 413s become routinized as a result of devitalization.

Really I sold my physical presence eight hours a day, five days a week, and my mind was my own twenty-four hours a day, seven days a week—my own for dreaming,

thinking, dozing, concocting fantasies. I received incre-
ments biennially, and, as a backstop, for the occasional
wild ride, so to speak, I had the money which my mother
and father had left quadrupled by now by Uncle Rob,
though I never let Barbara, whom I met at the office,
know exactly how much. Only because I was perverse,
she was addicted to the stuff.

Every payday the same dialogue:

"We have to try to get ahead, David."

"Yes, sweetheart."

"Money's nothing to be ashamed of, dear."

"Sure isn't, Barb. Wish I had a mint."

"A mint! A few more thousand added to what your
Uncle Rob has made for you, that's all. Dad'll equal any
amount you put up, he told me. He just doesn't believe in
putting the entire amount up, that's all."

"He's right, of course."

"You have to show responsibility."

"I agree. But I don't want to go into business, Barb.
Have absolutely no interest. Love putting index cards
into slots."

"You're a lazy slob."

"O, shut up, or I'll slot your slit."

Barbara was tall, easy-run, curvaceous, with round
breasts (36), brown hair, amber eyes, Miss America nose
(pert), long shapely rounded legs (shaved monthly), and
finger and toe nails done every other night (silver). O,
what a wonderful girl was she. I lie again. She was a
beautiful girl made of milk, eggs, and honey. When I
walked alongside her down the street and every man—
and woman—turned to look, I was exceedingly proud.
We made a handsome couple. We both wanted a home
and babies.

Yet as each year passed, she hated me with greater

124

passion. And I, her. Soon after I married her I realized she was a piece of dough stamped out in pretty configuration in an automated bakery. No, no, why should I insult the dead—she'd thought of herself as a pretty flower.

"Be gentle with me, David, I'm a flower, must be tended with care."

That's what I most wanted to do. To love her and be loved in return. I wanted neither a queen nor a whore—just a, well, a woman.

"Don't do that, David, it's dirty."

"What's dirty?"

"What you're doing."

I should have done it in her eyes and blinded her with darting spermatozoa. She hadn't wanted love, but to be potted and placed on the windowsill to be warmed by the sun.

Alicia, our little girl, had hair as blond as my mother's, a bouquet of wild golden mimosa, and a lovely bumptious little bottom that I loved to squeeze. But she was taken over completely by Barbara's Mother & Dad Co., Inc., their only child's child, and I had neither the courage nor the energy to fight back. She was my flesh, my love, my jewel, but they took her over and left nothing for me, so I had neither their daughter nor mine.

Totally and completely alone again.

Began to hope for a way out, and of course had one of those remarkable dreams people have about Barbara going for a walk and being hit by a falling gargoyle. Then her Mother & Dad retired to live in St. Petersburg, Florida, good riddance. Our marriage deteriorated to the point where I found it pleasant to go to the art museums to pick up girls as they gawked at Leger's metallic pistons and orifices. Barbara took up with Nick Dzrzschnzki,

125

a grab-bag of tenderness, sentimentality, repressed desire, genteel debauchery, a pacifist who loved gore, one of those defenceless creatures I had learned never to feel sorry for. When you first met him, you met a young man with a great bush of hair and beard—his first line of defencelessness. As soon as you began to speak to him, you found he answered from behind a hand which he leaned on and hid behind so that his words sieved through muffled and indistinct—his second line of defencelessness. Then as you began to make out the words you discovered they were enmeshed, surrounded, half lost, clutched in sentences of such circumlocution they were mazes even Theseus with Ariadne's thread could never navigate to freedom—the poor boy's third line of defencelessness. How sorry you felt for him when you first saw that pointy nose shining through all the hair, a pitiful airedale bemoaning his unappreciated fate. So you opened your gates to the man and awoke to find yourself in chains, overwhelmed by his hopelessness, his eternal wail at the cruelty of LIFE. I despise people who continually cry for themselves. That's an industry in which I hope to hold a monopoly.

While I picked up girls at the museums or the library, Dzrzschnzki came round to read his poetry to Barbara. To pulverize me because of my refusal to enter the conspiracy of making money (which I simply adore) with her father (whom I detested) she told me how Nick one afternoon forced her to her back and with viselike fingers (she even showed me the almost vanished black and blue marks on her thighs) pried her petallike legs apart as his nipper jutted hugely, she said (developing an astounding articulateness at my expense), and plunged it rippingly into her. Then, to really murder me, she added she'd come from the excitement of the rape. If true, it had been

126

the first time ever for she was as frigid as a wax gardenia in an icebox. As she had hoped, I became crazed at the thought someone else had slotted her no-slut slit and began to search for an old pistol inherited from my father. (It lies there in the drawer, coldly reptilian, at this very moment.) "And," she added quietly, "he returned the next day and the next, and I let him without fighting," and she literally licked her flowerlike chops in simulated lasciviousness. Mad with rage, the silly old gun in my hand, I went on a search through his usual haunts on Third Avenue, but after the third or fourth café, I said to myself, "Chump, what do you care who snipped your flower? You wish she were dead anyway."

One day soon she decided to take our child for a visit to Mother & Dad in St. Petersburg. At the airport I kissed my little girl, kissed Barbara, patted her behind (she winced), and said goodbye. They entered the jet and I departed to keep a date with Patricia Collins, a girl I'd met at the Wildenstein. We were drinking Bloody Marys, squeezing each other's thighs at some bar when the waiter put a TV on. A studio voice described an airplane crash and I was in the midst of saying "Turn the damn thing off" when I realized it was my family's flight.

I felt very calm and coldblooded about it. I paid for the drinks, said goodbye to Patricia, and walked toward Uncle Rob's rooftop apartment. I didn't think of Barbara at all. Just the insurance money. Yes, I did think of my little girl. But no tears at all. Cold as ice. As I walked towards the hotel, my lower lip cracked and began to bleed profusely. I didn't seem to mind as blood poured down my chin.

A doctor had to freeze my lip and suture it. It began to bleed again when I was told they couldn't find the pieces, not even one blond hair of my daughter's. Though I did smile when I realized there would be no burial expenses. Rob and Bry took care of me, especially two weeks later, after I tried to jump off the roof.

Gave up slotting IBM cards, since I was now, according to my standards, a rich man. The insurance came to twenty-five thousand dollars and I informed Rob's lawyer I would agree to the fifty thousand dollar settlement he had been able to reach with the airline counsel for loss of Barbara's services in bed and out, as he put it (how could he know she had been a flower who'd given nothing but a smell?), and pain and suffering for my daughter. Not a hair did they find. Not one thin, blond hair. So there I was, a rich man. Didn't even have to pay income tax on the money—just on the interest and dividends it earned for me after having been invested by Uncle Rob.

I took five thousand dollars and embarked for Europe, still more or less whole, if not wholesome. *Two souls, alas, do dwell in my breast.* Faust said that, but he was a conservative. At any rate, it was then I began to wear dark, tight-fitting, silk suits. I thought them extraordinarily becoming.

Heard Hamburg was the wildest town in Europe, so that is where I went.

It was in a dark cave of a *rathskeller* which backed up on a canal (Hamburg's as much a water city as Venice) that I met the dancer, Lillian, she of the mysterious center and the red shroud of a gown. She was a German *fräulein* who when in her cups liked to swing like an acrobat from the chandelier like a gibbet—gibbet?!—like a gibbon, a long cranial ape. Swinging from the chandelier, she'd cry, "*Steck es herein,*" swinging up and back like a she-ape, except she was no ape, she was one of those dark, thin girls whose secretiveness and darkness grabbed me in my own center. She went beautifully with my black silk suits. Seen in daylight, with my eyes wide open, taking inventory of her, I wondered why, but as soon as the sun went down and she touched my elbow with her thin, bony finger, my desire immediately became a clutching burning hand in my gut. She belonged to a powerful German fellow with a dreamer's eyes, soft blue, a strong jaw, and very unmilitary, blond haircut. He had numbers on his wrist but wasn't a Jew. Lillian told me that early in the Nazi take-over when the old Jews of Berlin were made to wash down the streets Kurtin stepped out from the jeering, sneering city mob, took the mop from an old rabbi and began to do the work himself. They sent him away but neglected to gas and burn him.

He and Lillian would visit one of those cellar cafés where the sex revolution had already seized power. De Sade would have been intimidated and immediately called for a turning back of the clock, merely from the overpowering smell of pot, malt, and alcohol, the bad jazz band, and the noise.

Lillian would become drunk and swing from the chandelier, her legs in a split, her mysterious center dark in the shadows. Though thin she had powerful thighs and my first thought and hope was to be squeezed to death by them. Kurtin, who it was said wrote plays, sat dreaming and drinking beer. Lillian excited and incited us, yet no one ever made a pass because we respected Kurtin, who could and often did stop a riot by merely rising from his chair and staring at the combatants. He had a way of making you ashamed of yourself by just looking at you, as if he'd read your marrow. Besides, he was very muscular and in top shape despite his many years, which were at least fifty. He rarely spoke, merely gazed into space dreaming, and drank his beer. When he did speak, it was quietly, almost in a whisper. If someone forgot himself and did paw Lillian, Kurtin would pick him up and throw him out the door.

There were times when I would drink too much and sit with him and he would ask me about myself and I don't know how many times I bored him with the same old story, but he'd listen attentively and kindly remind me if I continued to live without purpose I would become a massman, a nonperson, a dehumanized body, less even than any forest animal. When I would say that was all I wanted to be, an animal, he would merely stare me down.

Then he would gaze out into the semi-darkness of the cave, at the fake wildness of the scene, and, pointing to some man and woman under a bench or humped up in a corner, say, "Look at them closely and you'll see since their pleasure is public, contrary to popular belief, it is more strained, tauter, stylized, less free and less pleasurable. Public masturbation was a mass sport in primitive societies, a pleasant way to spend the afternoon, sprawled under the sun on the sour earth, but somehow we're not built for it. Tell me the truth," he once said, smiling, "have you ever enjoyed a good crap with someone sitting in the next booth?"

"No," I admitted, "but I haven't enjoyed it much privately either."

But, like all prophets, he wasn't listening, had to say what he had to say. "The more public, supposedly free, all this becomes, the less personal and the more violent it becomes, thus less free. We'll have to decide, you and I, on this matter, and soon. Otherwise we'll all be stark naked, out in the open, public, a spectator-player in a mass spectator-player sport—like those filthy swine," and he showed me the numbers on his wrist.

I really didn't listen to him, I wasn't interested. Inside I raged for his girl, to learn her secret, to explore her maze. I wanted what I wanted and right at this instant, now, exactly now.

And Lillian? She swayed in, she swayed away, she was mine, she wasn't, substance, nonsubstance, her center always in shadow, finite and infinite, a circle. And Kurtin spoke quietly to me, dreamed, drank his beer, and I pretended I was his friend, as her eyes caressed me, laughed at me, drove me on, turned me away.

Kurtin himself sent her to me. She herself told me. *They* hadn't gassed or burned him, merely smashed his scrotum between two bricks.

Up on my rooftop, again as filthy and stinking as a bear's cave, I lowered all the shades against night and day, lived on stale bread, refused to dress or even answer the door.

Tried to sleep, thought of Madeleine Dearing, wanted to run to her, to be sheltered by her, housed by her wifely veil, but shrugged with the knowledge it was all senseless.

In bed, staring into the dark, I thought of Taggart Strayhorn, of the miner with his toothless mouth as red as a clay pit, of Kurtin, of my mother, my child.

To escape thought, I took a couple of sleeping pills, but so inescapable is the escapable that no sooner did I fall asleep in my filth six hundred feet above *terra firma* than I had a dream.

I am alone on a road. The road goes I don't know where. It's a long narrow asphalt road from which nothing can be seen but the road ahead, nothing on either side, not even the horizon; neither the sun nor the sky are seen by me. Alone on a road, wary, biting a lower lip, scared, pretending I am fearless. I am aware only of the road ahead, long graded sill of concrete. I see myself a fist, all knuckles, tight, white bony eyes slitted under a forehead like a stone escarpment. Along this nothing road I stride alone, every step scattering a pile of discarded iron junk inside me, rusty edges scraping inner walls. My skin becomes tight, as sensitive as eyes, in the distance there are two figures. I begin to run towards them, faster, faster, but they elude me, and just as I am about to give up all hope, there they are. A man and a girl. She hides behind him as he turns to take me on, his fists on guard, confident of his strength. I step towards him and he raises a heavy fist, and I stop. He is in rags, his shoes tied to his feet with strips of tire tubes. Tall and powerful, his eyes gaze meanly, sharply, into mine. With my eyes I say, please, please, but I keep the muscles of my face taut. Don't beg, I cry to myself; neither beg nor cry or he will know you are afraid and then he will kill you. But he sees my grayness, his eyes held harshly, still he smiles and says it's all right, I can come along. The girl whispers in his ear, but he shrugs her off indifferently. She is very dirty, not a bad-looking girl even in her rags and dirty sneakers and torn tan coat with a cat-fur collar which stinks. I myself am dressed with great elegance. The girl nibbles at some seeds which she endlessly fetches from her pocket. The man is a dreamer, rarely speaks. The girl, after having come to accept my presence, becomes garrulous and gabbles on in disconnected words and sentences; obviously she is foolish. Once I call her Rosalind and she spits in my face. The man pays no attention to her or to me, he merely strides ahead between the girl and me. I

132

think about the girl. Cleaned and powdered, scented from the Perfumed River, she would be pretty, desirable.

The images vanish from my dream and I am very unhappy, uneasy, the weight is heavy, sharp, I can hear myself sigh. I turn the pillow to its cool side, punch it with my hand, urge myself to go off to a side to urinate, but again I am asleep and unhappily find myself with the girl and the man. She belongs to the man—his wife, his daughter, his friend? He is harsh and cold, yet when we pass a clear spring he asks the girl to drink first, then me, last himself. He must be a decent man, I say to myself.

In my dream night falls, black on black; I notice there are houses about, marble houses side by side with houses black with age, some gutted by fire. Shattered houses. The road has sides to it now, doesn't run through *nowhere* but exists in reality, and the sky has appeared, there is a slice of moon, yellowish.

Under an ancient black fir we make a fire and eat large sandwiches made of thick black bread and white pork. The girl and I dance about the fire, laughing, as the man, stretched on his back, stares dreamily at the black sky lit by a moon resembling an elongated lantern. Each time as I am about to catch the girl in my arms she escapes me. The man rests on his elbows and calls to her. They go off to sleep under a hillside ledge because apparently it is going to rain. I am very jealous and frightened and the weight is heavy. It aches and I remember something my mother once said. Loneliness is worse than a pain. *Lasciate mi morire,* I sing, hoping to make myself cry. I wish the dream would end. I lie with my head against the old fir and plan revenge on the man. I tread softly to where they are asleep, huddled in each other's arms. So vulnerable, so frail. Her face hidden in his chest, so I can't

133

see who she is, but his face is etched by the moon, black, white, gray. There is a tired, harsh bitterness in his lined, lean face, yet sweet from the smell of the girl's breasts. She turns about in her sleep and the light of the moon reveals her utter innocence, her astonishing frailty, and I wonder, is innocence evil? I bite my lip and it cracks and begins to bleed. I cry out with anguish, the pain inside me unbearable. Frantically I run to the ancient black fir and soon fall asleep in my dream.

When I awake in my dream, again there is the road, simply a road, no sides, no houses, no horizon, no sky. We stride ahead, the man, the girl, I. As the man pushes indomitably, powerfully, ahead, I look behind his back and catch her eye. She smiles innocently, sensually. She knows; she is wise, understanding completely that her circle is finite yet infinite. Obsessed with the girl, with the endlessness of her center, I am nagged by a nefarious dark night inside me. I plan an unspeakable crime.

I fight to rouse myself from the dream, work hard at waking and ascend to a space station halfway up between dream and wakefulness. On this orbiting platform I meet my blind friend with the purple meaty eyes. We exchange barbed pleasantries about our respective success in the grand world in which we live. He says, first reining in his dog so sharply it rises on its hind legs, "At least I got mine from my own pain, but you—" Angry, to get even, I pat his dog's head and grab a fistful of silver from the tin pie plate. But the coins tinkle and the dog snaps and rips my hand.

I am enraged and find myself running on the road, empty, nowhere, just a road in space; at each step I fly off the ground, leap, am weightless, and I wonder how it is I am carrying a club. The man and the girl sleep under the ledge of a hill, it is raining, and my feet are slogged down by mud. His face is bitter and tired, hers sweet and innocent, frail both of them, and I am choked with rage. I raise the club to strike him, to stave in his head.

I awoke with a cry and stared into the ceiling, into the gray darkness and faintly saw gold filigree and naked Tiepolo ladies—I was not fully awake—and began to slide back to my dream. A terrible oppressiveness weighted me down as I jumped clumsily from my bed. Awake now, still a remnant fantasy clung to my brain. I was an astronaut in a capsule to the moon, totally alone, silently whirring through space yet seen by half a billion people on their TV a quarter of a million miles away. I sat in my space suit, in full sight of them, vacuating into the chemical unit, a stupid grin on my face. The fantasy loosened its grip and my mind was free, left solely with its oppressiveness and the fear.

The dream, of course, in some measure had been a replay of the past and not a foretelling of the future.

Robe pulled tight, I found my way in the dark to the pot. Turned the flush, washed my hands, rubbed cold water into my face, brushed my teeth. Still in darkness I threaded my way through the debris of clothes, newspapers, dirty dishes on trays on the floor, to the refrigerator and a chilled orange.

Sucked on the half-sour fruit and stared into nothing. What is it we love? Ourselves? Is the woman we love merely a solipsist mirror reflecting our own want and need? Is it some woman we love or the female half of our own heart? Weren't Madeleine and I one, androgynous? Wasn't I conceived—romantic thought—precisely at the moment when Polly and Taggart became one soul with two hearts? *Two souls, alas, do dwell in my breast.*

And were not *they* David Strayhorn till the day he

died? Androgynous, double-humped, man and beast, the very devil with his two horns and his cloven hooves. No, not two souls. I was filled to bloating with every soul, man, woman, beast, which had ever touched me. If I stuck a pin into myself, out they would ooze.

I sucked on the sour orange as I sucked on my very own life.

We went, my harsh father and his smashed son, from London to India. I hated him for taking me from Rosalind, for being my father. For having said between clenched teeth, "Am I to be left alone?" Was I his keeper? Forever? A transient layer of pipe, he wandered the face of the earth and never turned his face toward home. "Home is where my wife was a whore," he once said. But he had left her, had he forgotten? A very human frailty of his. Not having the courage to face himself, he faced her, and not liking what he saw he ran. I was both he and her. He could look at me, his son, and both love and hate himself and her.

We learned over the years to speak to each other.

"Am I never to escape you?" I asked him once.

"No, never," he said. "It is the father who puts the spine in his son. Gives him the manhood to stand upright. It's the father who has to exert authority so the son learns he's not a wild beast, free to commit mayhem on all about him. You have to get it from me—who else?"

I could have told him a thing or two about mayhem but yielded to a generous impulse and didn't. "If I don't get out from under you, I'll be squelched forever. You're not strengthening my spine, you're breaking it. How will I ever learn to stand on my own two feet if you're always there like a crutch?"

"I'm not a crutch. I'm your mirror image."

136

"Then who is the father and who the son?"

"I am the father and you are the son. Accept it."

"I would accept it—if you accepted me as an equal. I'm not a child any more. Twenty's too old to be either coddled or beat."

"I've never coddled you or beat you."

"You've always had an exceedingly selective memory, haven't you? . . . Forget it. You didn't answer. If you accepted me as an equal, I could accept your fatherhood and be as filial as you want. There's nothing I ever wanted more than to be a son to my father."

"How can a twenty-year-old be equal to a man of forty-four?"

"You're getting into that business about the meaning of equality again. Excuse me. Accept my equal rights to be free. You go where you wish—I want the same right. I want to go home. To my own country. My own people. I want to go see where I was born, I want to see if it's true I wasn't born whole from the ear of a cloud. To go see if a kid I knew as Bash Balls married Nora Lynch," I laughed.

"You want to go to that *filthy* hotel." He'd said it a thousand times, and still the mention of it made him tremble and turn white.

"No, I don't. Though unlike you I carry no hatred in me about it. I make jokes about it to myself. I'm not going to carry it around with me like an oozing canker on my neck forever. Let me go, will you?"

"Not yet. I need you." He did not say it in a whining, begging voice—stated it merely as a fact, as one says I need food or water. That's all. Without either one dies. But I wanted to break loose. Be able to say I'm my own man. At last.

"Goddamn you. Can't I ever escape you?"

"Some day you'll have a son, you'll understand."

"Yes, I know. You've told me innumerable times."

He turned away, as he always did when we reached an impasse. It was infuriating.

"Even when I die," he said, "you'll not escape me. I'll always be with you. You're my son. Accept it."

"Happy to," I said. "But if I don't soon escape you, I'll die." Light suddenly entered my skull. "In the end that might be the way—to die."

And he sneered in his dark, harsh way. "A coward's escape." He always raged at the cowardice of others, since he was so obviously obsessed with his own.

I moved in front of him to stare straight into his eyes —my very own, agate gray. And sneered myself. "What is our life then?"

He clenched his teeth and balled his fists—he could still take me, the bastard—and strode away.

We worked together. Laying pipe. He reserved his greatest passion for just that. To neatly and efficiently drain men's waste, to hoard it or put it to use so it would not harm them. "What to do with our waste will become a greater and greater problem. Man's greatest blight." He was of course a prophet.

In India we worked in the field eight, ten, fifteen hours a day. Cholera and typhoid seemed to them a natural disaster. It drove him mad, and he worked obsessively. There was nothing he couldn't do, from planning, surveying, repairing tractors to laying pipe. The tractors we used were old and eternally in need of repair. Mechanics scarce in that impoverished land, he did the work himself, with his strong, agile fingers, and it was astounding how he could make an old dead motor sing. I admired him for it. Whatever he did, he did well. If only he had learned once to smile.

One late afternoon I was bulldozing. I had learned to love to drive a tractor—all that power under my ass. Gave one illusions. It was cool and I was wearing Rosalind's red sweater, daydreaming of her even though she'd written that she had married, which had made me cry. As I worked, the tractor engine began to stutter, to lose power, and in disgust I managed to drive it to the work shed. My father came out to see what was wrong. Still daydreaming, perhaps hating him, I shut off the engine, leaped off the tin seat, and sat on the ground as he tinkered with the gas line or magneto, didn't really notice. He worked quickly, efficiently, though impatiently, ripping skin off his knuckles and cursing. It didn't take him long and I started to stand as he inserted the crank in the old thing. There was something I knew I should tell him, but I couldn't bring it to mind. His muscles rippling under his shirt, he gave the crank a quick twist, the motor roared.

The tractor moved—Holy God, I'd left it in gear. I yelled, but too late, the machine threw him on his back. The front wheels, steel, crunched over his chest. His shriek could be heard over the motor's roar. I tore loose from my paralysis and jumped on the tractor, stopped it before the big, lugged rear wheels could mangle his legs. Ran madly to my father, whose breathing was an ugly rasp. He lay grotesquely unconscious, his face stone white, his chest cracked open, his blood running into the earth. I screamed and some men working in the shack ran out. They looked and winced. One hurried to the phone, the other to my father and me.

I sat on the ground under the belly of the tractor rocking back and forth; I felt nothing now, but heard a strange sound issuing from my mouth like steam from a slacking freight engine. My father was crushed, at every breath his chest a spurting fountain of blood. The workman stanched the blood with his shirt and towels he'd gotten from the shed. My father still breathed that ugly sound of rasp on rasp, towels sopping red. The man poured whisky down my father's throat, an ignorant layman's remedy for a man with a broken chest, bleeding to death. But my father opened his eyes. He looked at me, tried to speak. Just the rasp. I still rocked back and forth, feeling nothing, just seeing what I saw.

We were under the tractor and it dripped black oil on the blood. My father was dying and gazing at me with his gray adamantine eyes. I leaned over, kissed his forehead, and began to cry.

My father suddenly laughed, as if he'd won a big bet—I the loser—stared hard at me, sneered, and died.

And now I screamed, "Am I to be left alone?"

XIII

Patricide was my patrimony.

Neither he nor I was ever to be left alone. I hoarded him in my gut, somewhere between my crotch and lower intestines.

In the dark, sucking still on the already-dry orange, I pulled my robe tightly about me and walked out on the roof. There were the rivers flowing out to sea, silver and profoundly gray and black and ghostly. In the distance I saw the lights of a tug which towed a fleet of barges packed tight with shiny cars. Followed by another fleet laden with sand and gravel—the weight of the world inside me, heavy, sharp, and I leaned over the edge, sort of balancing my center of gravity with it.

Played this game for a while, seeing how close to making me topple I could roll the stone, rolling it back, then forward, back, forward, closer and closer to the edge.

No, no. Too easy. Took no courage at all.

Decided to sentence myself without trial to prison for murder one. Didn't plead insanity for I was perfectly sane, completely aware of every move. I was my own man, no one to blame, conscious, reasonable, and responsible for every act.

Moved into Uncle Rob's dressing room, which had a cot in it for the occasion he and the snake Bry had a fight. Another narrow bed in another narrow room.

Alone. Not one living soul did I see. Only the sun, the clouds, the sky, the moon, the stars, a plane in flight were my companions. On rare intervals I would permit myself to go out on the roof, like a prisoner permitted to do outdoor exercise, and walk to the edge. Quickly I would stare down the thirty floors to the street and crawling life. Terribly afraid, I would look quickly away and run into my room and lie on the narrow cot. The distance down was terrifyingly attractive. Surely that must be how hell had come to be invented. Some prophet with a stone in his belly, the stink of goat cheese on his breath, must have looked down into a rocky chasm and become frightened by how temptingly attractive falling all the way was to him, and discovered hell.

Drank water and ate stale bread.

By a natural selective process I first came to understand the constant drag of degradation one lived with in oneself, its heaviness, its yearning for the whip, and yet also the uniqueness of human life. Then came to understand the impossibility of grabbing hold of life, its retreat like a drop of mercury at one's touch, or, better, like a crab frantically digging into the sea bottom at any approach. But really life was a mirror image of oneself. It isn't life which is like a crab, it is oneself who frantically digs into the sand at the approach of life.

I sought out madness. Each day I crawled into a corner which would better conceal me, thus protect me, from the sight of the sun. I wanted to be mad because then I wouldn't be so maddeningly aware of every breath and thought and emotion. Somewhere I'd read that even when a man is mad he is conscious, at least in one corner of his brain, of himself, and that madness is at times akin to pretendiing madness—playacting that he is Napoleon or some such foolery and lucidly aware that he is play-acting yet doing so with such intensity he then does believe, like an actor, he is Napoleon or some such. Or, at night, all lights out, shades down, I would pretend I was a gray rat; I would grow a tail, my agate eyes would become beady, my sharp teeth would gnaw at stale bread, and I would silently scuff along the floor on all fours—and end up on my back, legs and arms poking stiffly above me, a dead rat, until I burst into laughter. No, I could be neither rat nor mad.

All a sham. To nurture this reality, I lit a thin cigar and puffed out my imagination: with my finger in the dust I wrote two stories on the floor:

I

A young lovely girl yanked herself loose from the clutches of a would-be rapist and loped down an alley smack into a broom handle. Nine months later she gave birth to twin whisk brooms.

II

An old man, wheezing and hungry, fell into a sand trap where he found and ate a golf ball. Thereafter, he lived from hole to hole.

Profound truth. Hahaha. Boom. Yes, yes. Hahahaha. Boom boom. Hahahahahaha. Boom boom. I rolled on the floor hysterically. BOOM BOOM! Haha, I laughed, if you're going to have a gas war—BOOM! BOOM!—haha, you better dintch the cigar. BOOM!

Rolling on the floor, hysterically laughing and farting, the shades swinging to and fro from the breeze, I knew I could not become mad. BOOM! BOOM!

A crowbar shoved up my ass the length of my spine refused me the comfort of kneeling to madness. And the crowbar protruded from my ass and curved under and forward and upward and beyond the arch of my body. I daydreamed of Madeleine being in the narrow cot with me. Amazing how a big fat girl—she was only a girl—like her could fit on the cot with me. We were so close the crowbar up my ass the length of my spine sort of grew and extended beyond the arch of my body. It became a rod of fire and not even peeing in the pot could cool it off. Then I fell asleep under the dying sun sliding down the Venetian blind, which simulated bars at the window.

Awake, I washed and stared at myself by squeezing my eyes shut so hard I saw an entire solar system of black suns and moons, then red space, then a void, then the image of myself, thinly elegant, dark, smooth, not a mark on my face, passing through life, untouched, all rock every part of me, and not even nuclear fission could undo my constipation.

Still the rod of fire protruded hot and heavy beyond the arch of my body.

Thought of Madeleine Dearing, of her misshapen obesity, her misfortune, whatever it may have been, and said, Look how slender and well-formed I am. Did I love her less? Perhaps for a lightning second, but then it was gone, the less defeated by the more.

Lolled about my cell—my room, what game did I play? —gazing into nothing or daydreaming of Madeleine. Sometimes I visualized her overflowing nakedness on the bed, her effusive thighs outstretched to reveal her hub, her circle, that repository for a man's end, his hope for endlessness, and his beginning. Her center sO expressively depicted in my mind's eye, I made callow, jejune jokes. So big, I said to myself, I can gallop through with a team of horses. Got with child, her huge paps filled with milk, I could exploit her and become a dairy ty-cOOn. That ham—what about some chow, old sow? Turned on her belly, she revealed a—

Broke off the jokes. I saw her spread across the bed, I at her side. We embraced and she drew me on top of her and with bliss I loved myself in her flesh, my cupped hands fondling her breasts with their large nipples, and I rolled on her flesh from side to side heavily, achingly, and she guided me into herself, and we rolled about, impressed ourselves indelibly on each other, and I was totally enthralled with the immense softness into which I sunk my hands, my body. Even after we spent ourselves we couldn't restrain our caresses, longer now, more tender, and then I fell asleep on her and she caressed my head lovingly, tracing with her fingers the convolutions of my ears, so that man and child were one.

As I slept, she kissed me, my slacked fingers, my head, my shoulders, until she herself slid into drowsy lethargy, and finally into sleep.

XIV

Made a jail break and the same incognito I took to chasing after Madeleine Dearing again. She accepted me on the old terms, the *cara mia* idiocy forgotten.

Mornings I waited for her to leave her basement apartment to go shopping. Soon I noted she bought less food. Was she on a diet? When I asked her, she merely shrugged, a stern look on her face. She only smiled when I took her hand in mine and brought it to my lips. I slavered over the hand like a thankful dog and she smiled brilliantly. She wanted me to be her slave. Who cared? When she smiled flashingly, the rock in my stomach became less heavy. Romantic poppycock, but I had to face up to it, romance was better than a tranquilizer.

Though she had apparently forgotten what she considered to be my insinuations, she was angry because I had not seen her for days and she refused to permit me to enter her apartment, even after I explained I had imprisoned myself for my crimes. I thought she would smile, but she shattered me with a stare of disgust, as if she were saying, "For God's sake, how long will this idiocy continue?"

"And yours," I mumbled, "and yours?"

She lowered her eyes.

She would bring me a sandwich and a glass of milk

and I would dispatch my repast while sitting on the shallow wall of her small, dusty courtyard, hemmed in by barred windows and doors and traffic-stalled cars. Then we would walk through the city to the concert hall. Every day, except on those when there were afternoon concerts, we would listen to the famous, near-famous, and would-be famous rehearsing; then there would be that one brief moment when she assumed the stage and shook the walls and cracked the weight in my heart.

When an identical routine is followed day after day, time moves rapidly because there are no side events to catch its eye and slow its tread, no park bench on which to rest or pause. Of course the weather varied, one of the delights of the temperate zone, as did the contents of the sandwiches Madeleine prepared for me—*mortadella, provolone, pâté,* pork sausage, Spanish onion, olives *judaico,* English mustard—the best sandwiches I had ever eaten. They enlivened me with a sensuous pleasure, as did the sun in its late spring yellow, the women in their lighter, more revelatory clothes, the children with their summer fantasies already upon them, the buildings casting softer shadows in their ravines, the touch of Madeleine Dearing's hand in mine: soft, tender, possessive, kind, wanting.

We walked through the streets hand in hand and, like her, I was completely oblivious to the constant rude stares of curiosity or ridicule we encountered—this huge woman and her tall, elegantly garbed—what? Lover? Brother? Husband? Who cared what they thought.

I had entered a time—it happens to everyone—when I overflowed with love and sensuousness, with kindness, romanticism, purity. Yes, I.

I loved myself. The same man who had seduced and forced a hairy porcine slob of a girl to her knees just a few short months before, the same man who had begun his pursuit of a fat lady merely cruelly to conquer her, who stole from a blind man, who sucked out women as though they were oranges, a fraud who lived with the compulsion to rob anyone fool enough to reveal his good fortune, and the unspeakable. The malevolent I found himself in a state of kindness and generosity.

Was it from the touch of Madeleine's hand, the love which softened her face (were my eyes deceiving me, was it only the blindness of ardour and adoration?), was it her patience with me which softened me, made me kind, warmly sensuous with the heavy scent of joyous sadness, which comes from great beauty?

I kissed her hands and she kissed mine. Between us always stood the iron door, squeaking on its rusty hinges, and her muteness.

One afternoon, lost among the many, we entered the concert hall while the full symphonic orchestra was rehearsing. Madeleine and I took our customary places on the center aisle steps halfway to the back and listened to the lithe conductor drive his instruments into a Berliozian frenzy. After numerous repetitions of a simple phrase, the orchestra took a break and while they were still rising from their chairs Madeleine rose and began to run, yes, run, to the stage. They all knew her, of course, and either ignored her or pretended to. The musicians were still straggling from the stage when she opened full throat. Everyone stopped in mid-air, and I stood without realizing that I had. As if she had picked up where she'd left off two years before, she was singing Desdemona's part of the love duet, the *quando narravi*, Verdi's passion, and her voice filled the hall, filled us, filled the sky and, I am positive, the earth. Perhaps it was right at that moment that the last stage of my love began. The beauty of her voice stunned me, my ears and skull thundered, and my heart opened and contracted to clutch the beauty in its furry claws.

Halfway through the aria she realized she was singing at last and broke off in the middle of a note, looked about, frightened, biting her lips, and we all stared at her for a few moments, dazed. Then we let go with cheers. The conductor ran, more precisely he sort of loped up to Madeleine and bowed deeply, took her hand and held it long to his lips. She withdrew, flying, gracefully too, the waddle abruptly gone, and I had to run quickly myself to catch her in the late afternoon crowds, as the buildings cast an oblique shadow across the street, like Adolf Hitler's bangs on the gray asphalt.

Deep inside me I cried out, Let her be, let her be, you'll be the death of her, but I had caught up to her and took her hand in mine and she raised my hand and pressed it hard to her breast, and in that fashion we rushed towards her apartment.

Soon we were at her door, she opened it and entered as I held it for her. She turned to welcome me and I began to walk towards her. She smiled brilliantly—truly, she had the face of an angel, a marvelously beautiful angel —and I stopped, stopped to admire her, and then there on the bleak stone inside me perched a black sharp-beaked bird croaking harshly. I wanted to scream with hatred at myself and at her. Wheeling, I slammed the iron door in her face and dashed insanely away.

Two days later, to my dismay, I received an envelope from her containing a letter in her grandiloquent hand and a sheaf of papers. I placed the papers on the round table alongside my chair and began to read her letter, but my eye caught the first words on the first sheet of the papers and I read along, stopped to read the letter, but was pulled back to the notes. Whoever it was wrote with a nervous hand, a hand in panic, but it flowed.

It follows:

My evil has different colors—one day it is the green of gall, another the blue of innocence, another the red of a knife's passage through living flesh. But the pain is all colors, unbearably blinding, so that the eyes of my heart must squeeze themselves shut. It is a devouring hell—a hell of splashing acid, drunk innocently, acid mistaken for water. A quick gulp and the pit is inside myself.

And she?

I've led her to the precipice and she doesn't even know how close to descending into hell she is. She's an innocent whom I love, as innocent as any child without the knowledge of evil, so she has been led to the precipice, having given me her hand in complete faith that I will not allow harm to touch her. Now she is at the abyss and soon will know the hell of shame.

The sea is the mother of all life. And after the new rebirth which we await so impatiently to replenish our world with genius and new insights, men will still say, the sea is the mother of all life.

On entering the city at noon, one finds oneself swallowed in the maw of a hysterical crowd. It has become, sadly, a holiday town. Then one realizes there is always a mirror about, a flawed mirror, so that it is difficult to hide, especially from oneself—the canals, quiet, lapping at marble steps.

This great city built by the most audacious of

men—to have dared raise this magnificent city against the challenge of the most immutable power on earth, the sea—this city has become a carnival town.

In its monumental square one is immediately impressed by the hugeness and repelled by the crowds and if there is beauty it is lost, for reality is lost and one does not believe the marble is marble but *papier maché*. Except for the *campanile*, which is an austere tower of brick. But the crowds are repelling in their greed, even though one has to admit that one too is part of the crowd—except, face-saving, one is different. Honky-tonk tunnel of love, the boats are more graceful, that's all. Cheap glass beads, cheap glass vases, the hawkers and gawkers are one greedy mob.

We have come for two days and immediately decide to cut it to one. She has come incognito and our sole pleasure is that no one has recognized her after her brilliant conquest of La Scala.

You enter your hotel off the great square, the clerks are smooth, pretty men, and an unease enters around your heart, pretty men with soft eyes and corrupt lush mouths. Venal. I've read too many books, I say to myself, and immediately forget about it. Your room is clean, you shower, your wife enjoys the bidet, and even that somehow gives you a spot of fear, as if the washing is a ritual ablution before sacrifice. Stop this foolishness, I say to myself; dress and go out to see the city.

Let's get away from the crowds of the square, I say, and we head back into the city; the *pontes* are interesting, the streets are narrow, the water lapping, lapping, the mirror flawed, everything about

151

you, including yourself, duplicitous. The buildings
are old with the coating of a million eyes; a huge
wooden door with graceful metal hinges is ajar, a
quick glimpse into cool marble *loggia;* the pretty
young men and the old caressing your wife's soft
body with their eyes, bold, carnal, and you feel
her respond to this Old World frank love of volup-
tuous women.

We turn a narrow corner, the canals are lost
from view, the marred mirror hidden, we walk
through some narrow streets, the crowds are gone,
all we see are the people of the city, and it is suddenly more substantial. We turn into a *campo,*
there is an old church, an old circular stone water
urn in the center, someone above, behind large
graceful windows, is playing an Albinoni cello
sonata, and you are directly entranced, and your
heart beats swiftly, and even your skin is alive as
it hasn't been forever. The smell, the sight, the
very air itself is a new sensation. Something in yourself is galloping.

The ages, those ages you have read about but
have never really believed in until this very moment, have worn the buildings' façades into an old
burnt-yellow color, so that there are no seams,
there is a simple ancient austerity, and the simple
old church has wiped clean the Byzantine garish-
ness of the cathedral; there is an ancient peaceful-
ness, this is the way it has been for hundreds of
years, and you are gathered into its arms.

You walk slowly among the old streets and you
come to the canals again, the *pontes,* the graceful
prows, the lapping on marble steps, the marble
façades worn, yet indestructible, the crowds

which you have already unconsciously decided to ignore, and the pretty, limpid eyes of the boys caressing your wife's opulent body, and you don't care, just a spot of pleasure at their pleasure in her voluptuousness which has always been just yours, and she is seduced and you are seduced, and with a rush, almost simultaneously, you both decide not to cut the stay short but to enlarge it, to stay on and enjoy the water city.

You wash, your wife again on the font, she smells of scent and something else and you turn your back on it, because suddenly you are both seduced by the old, by the carnality, by the holiday, by the crowds, by the boys' subtle smiles and frank dark eyes. They already sense—a sense which has been handed down father to son very much as the gondolier's craft has been handed down, as the glass-blowing craft has been handed down father to son—they know and sense and they have smelled as well as you have smelled, and they have marked her down. You turn your back because it is an evil of which you are aware and to which you are attracted and which you won't admit to yourself.

We dine and then go out into the square and mingle freely with the crowd and the water city's people, and I point out the sights that I know from fiction and from Ruskin. There's Florian's from Henry James, and there's Harry's Bar, and there's San Giorgio, and the Bridge of Sighs, and I tell her the story of Casanova's escape, and the Rialto, and the Grand Hotel, and the Palazzo Gritti. And her perfume is sweet and her scent, her very own, is warm and succulent, and now I am aware that that scent pervades the old worn marble, the stones, the quiet lapping water. I know the city is corrupt, there is no substance except the water, the sea from which all life has come, which has brought on its tides all the emptyings of the world's sewers to this city and its people have trapped it in their canals, for it is their only substance, it is their living, it is their bread and they nurture it with a hard cleverness which belies the soft darkness of their children's eyes, just as a Spanish peasant must nurture his sustenance on a rocky mountain ledge, for one must nurture what keeps one alive, and they have found their only sustenance is the sale of their worn marble façades, their canals, and themselves. We who have come to their city have brought our own evil to join with theirs, our own corruption to join with theirs. We have already fallen, I know, but she is unaware that we have.

We are tired from travel and excitement and return to our hotel room. We wash, and again I observe my wife's freedom of movement, her lushness expanding, her perfume and her scent, her ablutions which evoke this absurd unease and warm pleasure. Though tired, we make love, the wooden shutters open into a corner of the square, the breastlike Byzantine cupolas with their marble figures our sightless voyeur neighbors, the high heels of the women down below beating a staccato on the stones.

Refreshed, pleased with ourselves, elated, we descend again into the city. It is night, the water is a dark flawed mirror, and the perfume of women mingles with the odor of the canals, lush decay, worn marble, romantic poetic stars, lights playing on the soft, lapping waters, and the gondolier we choose is a young man, different from the clerks, powerful, deep-chested, with a robust beauty and the rollicking ways of a sailor, though all he has ever sailed has been his gondola and the only seas his canals—but his canals are the waters of the world, so he has sailed the seas, but he knows only the dark waters. He is a loquacious guide, his English more than adequate, but my wife speaks to him in Italian and they converse and laugh. An alien to their youthful concord, I stare ahead or from side to side at the fantastic shapes of marble night, hear the names Marco Polo, Byron, Pound, princes and princesses; and my wife sees nothing, she must turn to see him as he propels and steers the vessel with his magnificent single oar, and she is laughing as they banter and exchange quips in his mellifluous tongue. Though she seems to have forgotten I sit beside her, I know she hasn't forgotten because she has put her hand on my inner thigh.

My wife doesn't wish to hurt me, she is innocent and believes it is a sport permitted by marriage. She is merely flirting with the handsome young man—only recently have I seen reflected in her very own eyes my onrushing age—and I try to tear myself loose from the evil I fear is making her drunk with passionate excitement and me paralyzed—one small center of my stomach is pure vomit, and I attempt to enter into the banter between her and him, and I can see my wife has seen little of the sights, her hand on my thigh—for whose pleasure, mine? hers? the handsome gondolier's?

We return to the Ponte San Moise where we had begun, and I pay the fee, give the tip for he has given the tourist lady and her husband everything which has been asked for. We turn to leave, but my wife wishes to see the *pensione* he has told her about which is more beautiful than the hotel at which we stay and he takes us himself, which I can see pleases her. I want to cry out, to command her to stop, to tell her she is drunk with carnality and I paralyzed, attracted to the evil I can see playing about her full lips and darkening her violet eyes, and I am utterly in despair and the spot of vomit enlarges every moment.

We are shown a suite by a clerk, dismiss it between us, she and the gondolier go ahead into the corridor; I stop to thank the clerk who must close the room, and as I turn into the corridor do I see they had quickly moved apart or is it only some fantasy alive within me? They seem to be at ease and I join them, they are talking and laughing, and her voice is high, higher than usual.

Once again in the soft night, the flawed, rippled mirror before and behind us, we thank him for his trouble. He smiles frankly into my wife's eyes and she laughs gaily for no apparent reason except of course what is apparent only to me.

She is a quiet-spoken, gentle woman, really still a girl, of classical beauty which she carries off with a gracious dignity. But now her voice has become higher, her latent nervousness which she has always managed to check by a self-contained discipline—that selfsame obsessive discipline which had helped shape her into a great diva—has now seemed to free itself with a wrench as if she wished to tear loose from her gentle holdings.

She wished, I knew and understood, to taste corruption, to give it freedom of movement, as if unconsciously she knew that to live one must know the depths as well as the heights—it would make her a greater singer, a more profound artist—for without knowledge of the depths, the heights lose meaning, become a mere *longeur*. For me it appeared to be a disease of middle age, a last clutch at all life-giving opportunities which soon would be lost forever. Let me taste all life's pleasures before I lose the sense of taste. Let me have everything to remember, to sustain the decay of my years, and in that way ease the pain of knowing that what I have always put aside for another time has at last been tried. I must try for all, I must reach beyond the permitted, or I have wasted my days. What harm could come of it? As a young man I had tasted carnality, I had known the wry depths of my own evil. Only through her had I reached the heights. She is still a young woman, who has known the terribly arduous labor of forming and controlling the fine instrument which is her voice, the harsh labor of mastering her art and the cruel demands of her ambition to stand among the great. How high she wished to fly! Now she wanted to taste every food, every spice, wanted to try every smell and feeling. I knew she stood at the edge and wanted to fall and I had led her there confounded and confused by a desire to allow her to gain that knowledge over and beyond the lust sanctified by marriage. She must know—and I saw no reason for her not to know. But now I must ask, was it only for her? Did I also want to feel the indefinable exquisiteness of the knowledge of evil through her, to bring her to my own depths, so I could say, you too have known evil, are as evil as I, so that I no longer have to bear my evil alone because it has become too burdensome to carry alone. I will bring you down because you have been too high, too dignified, too arrogant of your youth, too innocent. (Was it also that I wanted to rediscover youth through another?) I had led her in the few years of our marriage through every garden, and we had tasted of every fruit and smelled every flower. Now we were passing through the final gate, to the garden where fantasy becomes reality and the knowledge gained is one which can only be borne by oneself—unsanctified, naked, cruel, brutal, overly sweet and murderous. It is an old lesson which every human being must learn for himself anew.

The canals smelled of urine and excreta and the *piazza* and *campi* and *palazzos* of carnal holiday —and I led her, my beloved innocent, to the market place where she wished to barter away her innocence and I to feel the frightening exquisiteness of sin through my astonished, wide-open eyes.

In our room again, as we undress, the open shutters reveal the cathedral figures immured in stone, cold-faced voyeurs. We discuss our calendar for the following day: we must see the sights, the palace of the Doges, the city from the crown of the *campanile,* the Titians and Tintorettos, the paintings of the brothers Guardi then at the Accademia and of whom we know little, I only from Stendhal's journal of his stay in Rome. We prepare again for bed, she astride the font as if it were a sacred pagan rite. So glazed are her eyes with excitement that as we talk she barely sees me; her voice is strident, her scent overwhelming. The spot of vomit in my center has grown to dimensions which fill the entirety of my middle-aged corpulence.

In the late night I awake and she isn't at my side. Before I even read the note, I know.

Tomorrow she will discover hell. Tonight, as I wait, I am already there. . . .

That's where Brian Lorimer's little journal concluded. I didn't need the rest, I knew the details myself. To quote a contemporary Russian, *Only when you have a venereal disease can you begin to comprehend how clean people are.* In Ariadne's lament which Madeleine had sent me she had underlined:

Tell me, where is the promise,
the vow so oft repeated?
The throne of thy forefathers,
throne where I should be seated?
The coronets of jewels
that should have bound my tresses?
Are these the shining sceptres,
the gemm'd and golden dresses?
Instead I am deserted. . . .

O Madeleine, O Madeleine, my love.

Dearest David,
Today I ached so without you my meagre rooms could not contain my pain, so I walked to the river's edge of this our island. My longing for you

was so terribly strong I felt you would know and be there, and three times it was you I thought I saw, but no, but no . . . I love you completely, tenderly, piercingly, irrevocably and you left me standing empty-handed when I wanted to give myself to you, to hold you sweetly in my arms. Ay, David, are you as afraid as I have been? If thou couldst see, O my love David, if thou couldst see how I am hungry but for thee.

I have become less afraid. I have spoken whole sentences aloud to myself as I stood before the mirror. I have become gross and yet I have seen you, my David, gaze upon me with love. This morning I sang many Schubert *lieder* and passers-by stopped to stare through my windows and some I saw were moved to tears. Ay David, today I brought Schubert's beauty to life and passersby cried. Yesterday, after I overcame the sadness of your having run away, I sat at the piano and sang Lucrezia murderously well. If you betray me, David, I shall poison you. Are you going to betray me? There are times when I believe I can see love in your eyes—but many more times I see cruelty and hatred. I shall never betray you, O David, for I have betrayed enough, but, please, my love, mostly I have betrayed myself. You must understand, you must, you must.

You know, David, I remember every word you have ever said to me. That was part of my training, to remember lines and music quickly. You are wise, David, and once as we walked about the city, you were chattering away and you thought I wasn't listening, taken with your own rhetoric as usual. "You were once very high and mighty, weren't you, Fatso?" David, you are so strangely cruel. "Then whatever happened to you and you discovered you were as frail as everyone else and as prone to dirt, it was too much to bear. The pure, great lady of the opera. It isn't what we do, is it, O Fatso mio, that hurts so much, but what it does to our own image of ourselves? Oo, that hurts. Just another human being, just another—" On and on you railed. At me? at yourself? Ah, yes, David, *dove è la fede,* tell me, where is the promise we make to ourselves to remember that we are but human? When I found I was no more human than everyone else, I became nothing to myself and swore eternal muteness. My tongue and heart spoke not, excepting to you, ay, David, my heart did speak. Hunger spoke for me, and the voice was sorrow's. It is true, I was so captivated by my greatness I could not see the flesh and blood around me. And you, my beloved David Strayhorn? You see the flesh and blood so clearly, you see it quiver and crawl and it has frightened you almost unto death, hasn't it, Mr. Blowhorn, my suffering braggart? O David, you see how contagious is your cruelty? Forgive me, my love, I have not the heart for it.

How strange, the more I come to life, the more I dream. The night before I sang from the *quando narravi* duet to you in the concert hall—it is to you I sing, no one else, for it is you I love, cruel David—I slept through two terrible dreams.

In the first I am waiting for my husband, we have an appointment but he does not appear. I am encircled by men and young boys who make their requests, some touching me, forming obscenities with their mouths, their tongues, touching, smiling, inviting, daring. I am distraught, angry with my husband because he also is daring me, that is why he has not come. I am frightened, my mouth is dry, my lips swell, and the men and boys become more insistent, drawing closer about me, touching me more intimately, and I find it difficult to deny them, to turn them away, and I hate my husband deeply, viciously. Where is he? He has become too old, I say quietly to myself. Then they are at me, like dogs, ripping at me, pulling, probing and I have become wild with passion and I am myself like a dog on all fours and someone is at me like a dog.

The huge square is empty, starkly empty and it is late night. The revelers have gone, the moon gleams whitely. I am lying on the stones, huddled in a corner, all alone. Cowering in a corner against the stones, the bell tower casts a frightening shadow over me; it is erect and cold as stone, impersonal. I am mute from fear and shame, a used dog.

It is snowing and I am strolling alone on a country road which snakelike follows a narrow river. It snows more heavily and I enjoy the winter white. I dance and sing along the river bank, I am a young girl. Two men approach me from out of the snowy night. They smile, wish to befriend me, but there is something odd about the older man, he is anxious about something, trembling, and I become fearful. The young man speaks softly to me, soothingly, and I am tempted, they are both handsome, but a finely exquisite fear from early childhood invades me and I begin to run through the heavy snow towards a house I see off the side of the road. It has become a blizzard. I approach the strange house and I am certain I have escaped them. The door is locked. Now the two men are upon me, breathing heavily, and the door does not open, and their hands are on me caressingly. I yield utterly, wildly. It is not me, it is my mother, and I am standing at the side, observing with a disinterested curiosity.

I forced myself to wake and escape from my bed.

You know, David, the following morning, after my husband and I were finally alone, the shutters shut to keep out the sun and the noise of the piazza, I lay on the bed exhausted, vaguely unhappy, seemingly impervious to all feeling, probably in a state of shock. I stood on the side, as in the dream, coldly observing as he paced about the room, nervously chewing his lower lip, his eyes unable to focus on me. As he packed his bags, I said nothing. When he left without even a nod, I said nothing. Did nothing; felt nothing.

For ten days afterwards I was two people, one frightened, exhilarated, yielding, the other a cold observer. Then late one evening in a plush hotel room, not mine, the two of me became one, and the man in the room was a total stranger. I couldn't even remember where I had encountered him. I went mad and had to be restrained by force from leaving the hotel and running about naked as any dog.

I heard nothing from my husband, or about him, until I was notified he was "killed" in a hunting accident in India. I mourned him. The enclosed notes were with his effects.

David, my love, my heart is open and speaks to

> you. You assaulted my heart with your obsessive
> attentions, with your cruelty, with your bravado
> fear, yes, even with your tenderness. When with
> your burning lips you kiss my palm I can feel your
> entire trembling body. Ay David, my tongue is
> speaking. And my heart. Soon, my love, soon you
> shall hear it. Thy wretched, deserted Madeleine.

My heart wept, yet my impulse was to burn her letter and his notes, and I even made a search for some matches. All the while I knew the impulse was fraudulent, I still played games with myself. Hide and seek. If I burned the evidence of their very human sins, I would by magical transference burn the evidence of mine. It didn't really matter whether I burned them or not. A fact's a fact like a man's a man. Every coward is hung by the noose of his past, which is an unburnable asbestos cravat. My tongue, protruding from my slack mouth, is swollen and purple. If the noose won't choke me, my tongue will.

Poor Brian Lorimer. Having led Madeleine to the Styx and introduced her to Charon, he chickened out and fled. In that hunting accident in Bengal, did he seek out the bullet or it him? And she? Now she wandered like poor Io the cow, and not even Prometheus could help her.

But I, like the Devil, could.

Still, I didn't wish to concede completely, she might accept it as surrender. She had, even I admitted, been betrayed enough. But above all I did not wish to betray myself. So I wrote a snow-flaky lie and sent it off by messenger.

> Madeleine, my sweet little pig, I am ill. Please
> come to me. Hurry. David.

XV

When I opened the door in answer to her knock, a lascivious, crooked smile scribed her angelic face. We simply, and silently, fell into each other's arms (hers were astonishingly strong), the room oddly pervaded by an odor of fog, fresh, heavy fog. I felt myself drawn into the center of a wildly whirling wheel from which I was unable to fight myself clear, so I let myself go. We were quickly in a breathless embrace, the silence broken only by the pounding of iron into hub.

We breathed heavily, peacefully, and I felt alive. She smelled of fresh dampness as I sprawled on her hugeness, spent, sweetly alive.

Slowly I became aware of the world. Could hear the watch on my wrist, ticking. Could hear her heart through her breast, beating. Could hear a jet plane, whistling. Underneath her, my hand on the hard floor became numb. I itched at my crotch. Her largeness beneath me was an affront, her odor distasteful. The touch of her shriveled me. I was sad. Fought against being repelled, but that dredged up nausea, and I knew I had to leave her. So she wouldn't feel rejected I left her gradually, releasing my hand, slipping from her to lie alongside, but she held on tenaciously, and I became angry.

Broke her hold on me, rose to my feet. Hurriedly I

165

gathered my clothes which were sprinkled about the room, as were hers, and began to dress. She regarded me with shame, then like a huge white animal she crawled towards me, her udders almost touching the floor, and held me by the legs. I despised her.

"Go away," I said quietly; but she hung on, gaping up at me. "Go away!" I screamed because she made me act like a movie villain, the cad kicking the good girl who had fallen. She held my legs tighter, her breasts soft against me. But I couldn't bear the touch or smell of her, and I slashed down at her. She slumped away with a gasp of pain like a mute animal beat with a club, and I headed for the sliding glass door to the roof.

Behind me I heard the wet gurgle of a tongue stuck to a palate, the gagging of a throat on a word which never quite formed. Like a bone it choked her.

I looked about at her. Her entire body was writhing with the effort of speaking, blown up with the word which would not form and be spoken—she was all tongue, saliva, and compressed breath. Her face became swollen and purple with effort. And her eyes pleaded with mine for compassion. I felt none and could give none. I was a stone. I turned away as hopelessly she sank to the floor.

Stood at the edge, avoiding a downward glance, afraid to look, afraid of the temptation. Madeleine and I possessed one another now—no doubt about it, but I was afraid. I needed courage, but I was a coward. And my disgust was not for her but for myself.

My back to the parapet, I saw her through the glass door rise heavily to her feet and walk nakedly, slowly, to the bed. It sank almost to the floor as she climbed into it, huddled herself together, cowered, squeezed herself into a corner of it, as if to die—that overflow of human flesh.

When she had grasped my legs, looking most hopelessly fat and lost, I had most wanted to beat her with my fists. When a victim asks to be beat, who can be so cruel as to refuse? Yet I felt an infinite tenderness for her, too, and my only desire was to caress her wounds and sorrows from her insides. She was, I felt, as capacious inside as out and for that I loved her. She had room for my entirety—there were no narrow corridors to squeeze my soul and low-hanging beams on which to knock my head. How different from me. My insides were cramped for space, a pinching narrow space, room enough only for my very own stone and nothing else.

By the light of a small lamp near the bed I could see the white hump that she was, rising and falling in the slow rhythm of sleep.

Courage flowed into my veins and I could turn to look down into the dark depths. The dizziness thrilled me. Down below was salvation. I leaned over, far over, and the weight inside me began to roll towards my head, to change my center of gravity. Soon, top-heavy, down I would tumble at the rate of thirty-two feet per second per second through the air like an aerial artiste, doing front flips, back flips, double flips. Within an hour a department of sanitation man would wash me off the sidewalk with a hose. How refreshing.

If I were to fall all the way the rock would come to an end, since I had no heir. Smash would go the stone into a million pieces. Some poor bastard down below might get a gleaming chunk in his eye, which would soon miltiply. He would then pass on rocks in the head to succeeding generations. At least my line would be through with the cursed thing. My line would be through, period.

I stood at the very edge, leaning far over. I felt very quiet inside. No churning, no tumult, no lack of energy, just quiet. Why at the very moment I stood at the edge?

Must I find serenity only now? A man lives his life, I thought, with all its busyness, its conundrums, its manias, and he never stops to wonder if he has lived at all. It has never occurred to him he hasn't lived or he wasn't then living. Then he's caught up short.

This is no way to think standing at the edge. Step back, get into the room, quickly, I command myself in a very cool, quiet manner to avoid any possible panic. It must be without fear or hysteria, it must be with pure reason, voluntarily, freely. But my body remains immobile as if it refused to concede there could possibly be anything to be scared of.

I look down and see tiny men and women scurrying about. And I am leaning over as far as I can without toppling. And I am thinking I have always concealed myself—that is the secret of my malaise, that I have always hidden in vast preternatural corridors and shadowy cellars. I had learned as a child that to reveal my inner feelings was to expose myself to the sharp edge of contemptuous silence or quizzical contempt. In those late mornings in the *hotel* when most of the help was asleep, when I would ask my mother, as children do, to explain why I was or how or what, she would either slap my face or play the tinny hotel piano. When she played I knew even as a child that she was burying herself in her own vast tinkling horror. My father, of course, had considered any talk about who, how, or what as being emotional and would at the mere suggestion of a question raise his heavy black eyebrows and flare his hairy nostrils. He was an engineer. Odd—or is it not odd?—that I should now fall in with a woman who conceals herself in muteness and a barrel of fat.

So now I stand at the edge, it has come at last, and I

look down, wondering if it is worth it, that's all. Is it all
or any of it worth it, and wondering if this just-discov-
ered seriousness isn't also a concealment, to hide from
what I now most wanted to do, to hide the way a child
hides under the blanket in his fear of the dark, becomes
more frightened and presses his eyelids tight, tighter, until he sees the falsely induced stars one sees when one
presses one's eyelids hard together. It would seem simple
to escape the burying blanket and dare the dark for a few
moments and stand at the window to observe the real
stars in their flight—or, simpler, less poetic, to dare the
few dark, frightening steps to the light switch on the wall
and expose oneself to man-discovered light and then to
smile at one's own silly, embarrassed smirk in the mirror.
The mirror image would perhaps observe a frailty, a vulnerable tenderness.

Can I be trusted to stay the knife of death at the naked
target under my very own heart?

No, I say, taking one step closer to the edge. There
is no more to go. I have not dared face the risk of living
for so long that now I stare into the deep, howling, very
hard face of death. I stand at the edge of the roof, the
moon a glow worm, and stare down to the street and
become frantic, and becoming frantic I can still wonder
at the revealing thought that life and death are kin, very
real kin, all else superstition. One more step to nothingness, that's all. Go now. Somehow I manage a tight smile,
enough of a smile so my parched lips crack and I can
taste the blood.

Father would have sneered, "emoting again?" then
turned his harsh face to the wall, towards nothing,
snarled, "You can never escape me—or her with her
whorish blood." My mother would have slapped then

169

cried or cried then slapped—no, no, I whisper to myself, if you're going to go, go, and on your own. Your very own.

I stand at the edge and do not feel the wind or even hear its howl. It is up to me alone.

I look down the full six hundred feet of the pit to the asphalt paving. A touch of vertigo makes my head reel, and an even quicker desire to let myself fall all the way into that pit pushes me till there is no further to go except down. And I am not I but some other person whom I am observing and I know that is very bad. Still my head reels and it is my heart beating and not his, my stomach nauseous, not his, and the paving at the bottom seems to rush up to meet me coming down, and I am letting go and crying NO! for soon I will be a splotch of bone and blood.

And I hear the cry, "DAVID! DAVID!"

My heart pounds in my ears. And I hear myself laugh a hysterical laugh. And it is too late to fall.

I looked through the window. Huddled into a corner of the bed, Madeleine was fast asleep, and the part of me dissociated from myself laughed again, and I re-entered the room. There were moments when I was certain I *was* crazy, but I knew that was only an alibi I'd been trying to fabricate to get me acquitted. Of what? I wished neither to plead guilty nor to prepare a defence of insanity, nor, yet, to force an abdication of reason. What I wanted, I suppose, was to plead *nolo contendere,* to be guilty without admitting it, *since the only thing I felt guilty of was being alive.*

As for my small, very banal evil acts, I drank them like the purple square his whisky, machinelike, with no guilt. The simple fact was, I liked them.

In the room again, I ogled Madeleine Dearing asleep on the bed. I slung myself across a steel so-called easy chair, an idiot of a chair, steel square skeleton clothed with a leather apron on which I could lie suspended, neither comfortable nor easy, sort of a modern rack whose purpose was to suspend one between unease and torture. Take your choice. God forbid one should have even a moment's ease. The room was a rat's nest of shredded newspapers, bad odors, in complete disarray from my having holed up in it, long ago having forgotten how to live in it.

Madeleine, my obese lady, barely breathed, only slightly contracted and expanded, a half-dead thing. Outside it began to drizzle, a dismal gray night sky overshadowed the city, the roof on which my grimy windows dully stared smelled of musty old tar, and from far below I could hear the customary harsh squeal of tires, honking of horns, explosions of faulty carburetors and rusted exhaust pipes, an occasional cop's shrill whistle. Not so far below, really, only six hundred feet to cement bottom, except that down below was death and that was very far since up here enormous Dearing and *doppelgänger* I still managed to be alive. Even in that dubious state, *just alive*, death's very far.

There she lay, a half-breathing, half-dead lump, on my disheveled filthy bed, a scarlet welt on the side where I'd so harshly struck her. Though she'd lost thirty pounds for love of me in the past few weeks, still she was quite a large piece of baggage, and I could hardly believe that not very long ago she had been a lovely, opulently beautiful girl with the innocence of Eve before the fall. She had remained innocent so long one wondered if she weren't a fool. How could anyone live beyond the age of pubescence and still remain innocent? Her husband had pushed her, it's true, but since she'd not fought back one could easily believe she had taken her pratfall willingly. Spread out on her elegant can, an open target, a couple of *venezianos* had slotted the bull's-eye without even taking aim. They had done nothing to boast about. Fallen at last, driven from the paradise of her naiveté by the suddenly acquired knowledge she was just plain mortal, her scream had become a mute cry, the cry of a dumb beast which has lost its voice. *I am a beast*—cried Io—*that frenzied/ runs with clumsy leaps and bounds,/ oh, shame,/ mastered by Hera's malice.*

How we're driven, I thought, by our punctured fragilities, our violated vanities. As if in her unconsciousness she had read my thoughts, Madeleine sighed deeply, expanding like a balloon with the intake of air, contracting with its expulsion, the bed sighing too, pulsating. Soon the bang!

Bestirred myself from the steel uneasy chair, stretched my lean rat's length, yawned to reveal my sharp white teeth, padded over to examine her more closely, intimately. Earlier I'd covered her nudity with a white spread since I wasn't one who believed in public display of what was private—a virtue just recently acquired anew by the lady and myself, too late acquired, almost fatal. Like one of Newton's laws of physics, in human life too perhaps every action has an equal and opposite reaction.

Her feet under the white spread were in the first position, in comical Charlie Chaplin style, and the spread pressing down on her was embossed with her triangle. I couldn't escape it. Unable to restrain my hand, I lovingly caressed her where the mound showed. I stared at her, searched her sleeping face. Though her body had become gross, her face had retained its sensitive yet young sensual beauty, a long oval face with a classical Greek nose and strong nervous lips, blood hungry as Medea's, and a high, gently curved forehead framed by a loosened mass of reddish-blond hair. The Venetian boys, I was sure, had followed her about as if she had been one of Titian's fabulous pagan nudes stepped off the canvas to promenade along the Grand Canal. I examined her face and felt myself smile at the mustache of sweat drops like tiny sea shells strung along her upper lip. I turned to look for something, my hand reaching in space, then laughed loudly at the realization it was for a pencil with which to make the mustache black. Stopped the laugh in mid-octave and observed the face of my burden, my dearest Dearing, with an empty feeling in the center of my stomach—what comes next? and soon sadness overtook me, and, kneeling, I placed my head on her breast, soft sweet breast, with the hope the rhythmic surge of her sleep would ease my heart.

Instead, like a wild dog, I howled.

She awoke to stare into my cowering eyes, to caress me gently, with a tender patience, to wipe away my tears with her soft fingers, but I felt her love asked too much of me. She opened her arms wide to beckon me, to take me to her, the love in her eyes brilliant, too brilliant for my naked eyes, and, in self-protection, I again struck out at her. A red blotch spread over her face. She groaned and her body quivered with pain. But her arms held me strongly, remorselessly. Three inches from her, I stared into her eyes. I felt a throbbing in my temples and I tried to leave her, but I couldn't—she held me in a vise. I tried to look away, but her eyes commanded mine. They had changed radically and swiftly from love to pain to something new, something I'd never seen in them before. They had become hard, strong, and I could now easily imagine how she'd worked so obsessively to place herself among the immortals. She breathed heavily from her effort, her breasts rising and falling against me. Her arms held me like steel bands. And there was something odd about me that I couldn't understand, a sense of change, too, as though I had broken loose from the magnetism of the earth's core and was floating in space. My lips thickened; my body became a mass of twisting, jittery nerves. It was as if whatever it is in a man's head which keeps him un-der constant surveillance had been shattered, and I was without guidance, floating in mid-air, free. I wanted to turn away from her eyes, they were relentless, mad, but my steering mechanism had come loose and here I was traveling at the speed of sound. My heart pounded wildly. And she held me with all her weight, two hun-dred pounds pressure per square inch; we were so close we were truly two souls in one breast. We wrestled for life, cruelly, graspingly, unyieldingly, in utter silence but for the lisping sibilance of surging breath escaping slit lips.

Finally, with a monumental tearing I broke loose from her, thought I'd made my escape, but with a fat swiftness she bounded from the bed. With the total strength of her greatness, her heart at last bursting the walls of its im-murement, she came at me with flailing arms. Befuddled, I tried to encircle her to contain her wrath. I held her so tightly I thought my blood vessels would rip and my muscles shatter. Her anger, communicable, alive, infected me, and my very own anger now shook me by my heels. With a howl and a last-chance remnant of strength I threw the single struggling body that we were down on the bed. It teetered, pulsated, came apart with a bang. We saw stars, a new solar system was born. Our orbit one and the same, we stared agape into each other's astonished face.

Our laughter began in our bellies and worked its way up. When it came out it was half lamentation and half hysterical relief. As if we'd just been saved.

We were quiet.

We embraced.

We kissed.

Between us the air pulsed in cataclysmic excitement. We spoke.

Madeleine. David. My fat little pig. My skinny horn. An onrush of words, interrupted by more kisses, another embrace. We swore undying love.

Later, stretched out on the broken bed like a contented lord, I admired her as she stood atop my round oaken table in an opera star's stance. As I gazed up at her in all her glory, she appeared tall and majestic, her hair about her shoulders, a tender yet arrogant smile playing her hungry lips, her great breasts alive, her buttocks and hips bulging, her belly round over the reddish-blond curls which hid her mysterious center, her thighs forming a monumental ogival arch. She sure was a big fat lady. And as she raised her head and opened her mouth to sing, I remembered that first time when I crouched in the cement courtyard peeking through her iron-barred window how hopefully my ears had strained to hear the beauty of her voice. All her dignity, all her hopes, all her humanity would be in her voice—all to counterbalance the beastliness of her flesh. And she—and I—would be redeemed by that beauty. I would hear her soul, and between us would be communion.

So now, as then, my mouth opened in expectation, my eyes glittered, my lungs panted, my thighs became weak and in my groin I felt a delicious fertility. She shifted her feet, raised her arms, closed her eyes, cocked her head as though listening to the orchestra for her cue, and, forming her lips, she let go.

About William Herrick

William Herrick was born in 1915 in Trenton,
New Jersey, moved to New York City at an
early age, and was educated there. He is offi-
cial court reporter for the U.S. District Court.
He is married to the former Jeannette Wellin.
They have three children.

Mr. Herrick's first novel, *The Itinerant*,
which was published in 1967 by McGraw-Hill,
received excellent critical attention. He is at
work on a third novel, to be published in
the fall of 1968.